Through The Looking Glass

Collections In Miniature

BY ANN RUBLE

Ann Ruble
2454

BOYNTON AND ASSOCIATES, INC.
CLIFTON, VIRGINIA

To—
Catherine B. MacLaren without whose foresight and determination there would be no basis for this adventure, and to Bonnie Schroeder who filled the editorial gap and allowed me the time to write this book.

Printed in the United States of America, by Benton Review Printing. Text pages designed by Jack and Kathy Gordon. Covers designed by Randall Vlahos. Art production by Jan Gilliam and Mary Devaney.

Unless otherwise noted, all photographs are by Nutshell News photographers Chris Becker, Shelby Harris, Jill Riner and Olive Rosen, or by Nutshell News staff Sybil Harp, Ann Ruble, and Bonnie Schroeder.

Cover Credits: The dollhouse on the front cover was loaned by Dotty Jacobs, Minis From The Attic, 2442 N. Harrison St., Arlington, VA 22207. Model: Betsy Boynton. Photo by Chris Becker. The parlor room on the back cover was designed and executed by Nic and Linda Nichols and can be seen in the Miniature Museum of Kansas City collection.

Contents

Introduction

A journey through the world of miniatures is much like Alice's adventure through Wonderland: It is a world beyond the Looking Glass where all manner of amazements will greet you. It is a land where reality and fantasy exist side by side, a place where both children and adults can "play" creatively and thrive in a world of their own making.

Miniatures as we know them today encompass a wide range of interpretations from small paintings and books to dollhouses and their furnishings. For the purpose of this book, we will concentrate on dollhouses and similar small scale dwellings.

Although children have always enjoyed dollhouses, many of the small, elaborate domiciles mentioned on the following pages have been more appropriate for adults. These miniaturizations of a larger lifestyle have fascinated adults for centuries. Miniatures have existed ever since primitive man first carved small figures from stone to represent his gods and idols. Centuries later, tribal cultures continue to use miniature replicas in their religious ceremonies.

As part of a religious ritual, the Egyptians fashioned miniature versions of life's necessities for placement in the tombs of their rulers. It was believed that these small objects assisted the dead during the After Life. Because the Egyptians were fascinated by beauty and craftsmanship, we can surmise that they took great secular pleasure as well as religious satisfaction from these miniatures.

The evidence of miniature objects used either for religious purposes or as playthings can be traced throughout history. While an interest in miniatures among the Romans and Greeks is less specifically documented, some pieces of small furniture have been unearthed in these lands, suggesting that the children of Caesar and Plato also played with dolls in room settings or dollhouses.

A major interest in dollhouses sprang up in Germany in the 16th century. The oldest fully-documented dollhouse built in Europe was a four-story mansion commissioned in 1558 by Duke Albrecht V of Bavaria. Originally intended as a gift for his daugther, the Duke kept the house for himself, adding it to his art collection.

In what was perhaps the most ambitious miniatures project undertaken until the 20th century, Duchess

Augusta Dorothea of Schwarzburg Gotha worked throughout her 80-some years to create a miniature version of her world.

She called on the most skilled Court artisans to build 26 model houses, 84 rooms and 411 dolls depicting daily upper class life in the period between 1670-1750.

From Germany, the fever for dollhouses spread throughout Europe. The marvelous toys which came from Nuremberg, the toy capitol of the world, delighted adults as well as children. Monarchs visiting Germany were inspired by the toys and dollhouses they saw there, and they hastened home to commission their own miniature dwellings.

While the Germans built dollhouses, the Dutch preferred "cabinet houses," elaborate cabinets with doors whose interiors were divided into cubicles or rooms. The doors kept theminiature treasures hidden when they were not in use, and the cabinet style blended with the rest of the home's full-size furniture.

The French described their dollhouses as "maisons de poupees," a literal translation. Queen Marie Antoinette brought her dollhouse with her from Austria when she married Louis XVI. She later gave her own children a dollhouse.

The English referred to their dollhouses as "baby houses" and often had the estate carpenter duplicate the manor's full-size furnishings in miniature for these houses. Queen Anne gave her godchild Ann Sharp a baby house which has remained intact in the same family for three hundred years. Prince Frederick, the Prince of Wales and father of George III, sometimes occupied his leisure by building dollhouses. The young Victoria also had a dollhouse, although it was much less elaborate than those owned by other royal children. After years of being considered primarily an adult novelty, it was during Victoria's reign that dollhouses were reinstated in the nursery as a beloved plaything.

The Colonists brought the miniatures tradition to the New World where it has continued to flourish. Appropriately, the first documented American dollhouse was a simple Early American style house built in 1744 for children from a Boston family. Many years later, President Rutherford Hayes' children played with a dollhouse during their years spent in the White House. Dollhouses and miniatures figured most recently in

White House Christmas decorations during the Carter and Reagan administrations.

Trying to understand the fascination with miniatures is almost as intriguing as viewing the elaborate and astonishingly realistic furnishings and houses themselves. The explanations for this interest in small scale objects are as varied as the miniatures which comprise the hobby.

As a hobby, collecting and making miniatures satisfies a variety of creative and emotional needs. For many people, small scale objects satisfy an intense urge to collect. The artistry of a piece speaks to their sense of beauty, and the miniature's precision intrigues them. No doubt there is also an element of competition among collectors: Who can discover the best, the most unusual or realistic, the smallest, the newest, or the most expensive miniature object?

Many small scale objects are works of art and are appreciated, collected and valued as such. Dollhouses also act as wonderful documents of social history. Peer into a 19th century dollhouse which has remained intact, and you can learn how the inhabitants lived — and by inference, how the owners of the dollhouse lived.

As works of art and documents of social history, miniatures have found their way into the collections of the Metropolitan Museum of Art, the Smithsonian Institution, the Chicago Institute of Art and Chicago's Museum of Science and Industry, Amsterdam's Rijksmuseum, France's Musee des Arts Decoratifs, England's Victoria and Albert Museum, and countless other regional and local museums and historical societies.

Thanks to their ability to document the life and times of their owners, dollhouses help us recapture the history of an age, or perhaps the personal history of certain childhood memories. Miniatures offer us a chance to create a controllable environment and realize our own dreams. The miniatures world is a place where all things are possible because there is no limit to the self-expression available through this hobby and art form.

As Alice discovered during her journey through Wonderland, this smaller-than-usual place is one made for dreaming and learning, but most of all, it is a place meant for enjoyment. Come, step through the Looking Glass, and let the fun begin.

Ann Ruble
Fall, 1984

Acknowledgements

The Editor and Boynton and Associates Inc. thank the following authors, publishers, and agents who granted their permission to use quotes found in this book. Every effort has been made to trace the ownership of the selections included and to make full acknowledgement of their use. If any errors have inadvertently occurred, they will be corrected in subsequent editions, provided notification is sent in writing to the publisher. Many of the works included are traditional, and the authors are unknown.

Dodd, Mead and Company, Inc. for "In the Bazaars of Hyderabad" from *The Sceptred Flute* by Sarojini Naidu. Published in the Dodd, Mead and Company book *Favorite Poems Old and New*, by Helen Ferris. Copyright 1957 by Helen Ferris Tibbets. "Vagabond House," from *Vagabond's House* by Don Blanding. Copyright 1928 by Dond Blanding; renewed 1956 by Don Blanding.

Harcourt Brace Jovanovich, Inc., for "The Secret Cavern" from *Little Girl and Boy Land*, by Margaret Widdemer. Copyright 1924 by Harcourt Brace Jovanovich, Inc.; renewed 1952 by Margaret Widdemer. Reprinted by permission of the Publisher.

Macmillan Publishing Company, Inc., for "Barter," by Sara Teasdale. Copyright 1917 by Macmillan Publishing Company, Inc.; renewed 1945 by Mamie T. Wheless.

Oxford University Press, for "Plum Trees," by Ranko, from *A Year of Japanese Epigrams*, by William N. Porter. Copyright 1911.

Grateful acknowledgement is also given to the following people who assisted the Editor in the preparation of this book; Mary Devaney, Jan Gilliam, Jack and Kathy Gordon, Sybil Harp, Myrna Hopkins, Carol Kulenguski, Catherine MacLaren, Bonnie Schroeder, Susan Sirkis, Dee Snyder, Phyllis Tucker, Randall Vlahos, and Thyra Weeks. And special personal thanks to David Molpus.

Personal Favorites

Long after an article is written and photographs are taken, long after the parts join to become a complete feature published in **Nutshell News**, and long after specific details have become mere recollections, the images and feelings the work evoked live on. In this sense, an artisan's work is timeless. There are certain rooms, houses, figures which remain vivid in the mind because the emotion they stirred lives on in the heart. In preparing this book which represents some of the best work featured originally in the pages of **Nutshell News**, the editors of the magazine were asked to pick their personal favorites — miniatures which for whatever reasons illicited this type of personal, emotional response. Their choices, and their reasons for choosing certain settings, are as diverse as the people who make up the **Nutshell News** staff.

The character of **Nutshell News** has been shaped by the people who read it and the people who put it together each month. Without the foresight of Catherine MacLaren who founded the magazine in 1971, there would be no publication which so completely addresses the interests of miniatures collectors and craftspeople. Without the help of many fine hobbyists who have contributed their talents and knowledge to the pages of **Nutshell News**, the magazine would not have continued to grow, improve and meet the changing needs of miniaturists worldwide.

Nutshell News is fortunate to have a diverse group of hobbyists on the editorial staff. Managing Editor Bonnie Schroeder, Associate Publisher Sybil Harp, Special Projects Editor Bonnie Bennett, and myself, Ann Ruble, comprise the backbone of the editorial staff. Bonnie Bennett, an active craftsperson, works out of her home workshop near the NN offices. Associate Editor Dee Snyder, who has been with the magazine since its infancy, writes, conducts miniatures workshops and offers observations on miniatures from her home in Florida. Founding Editor Catherine MacLaren is active in the miniatures and doll collecting worlds and keeps her finger on the pulse of miniatures happenings in Southern California — where the hobby as we know it today was formally acknowledged over 10 years ago with the formation of the National Association of Miniature Enthusiasts.

Each editorial staff member is a confirmed miniaturist, although our tastes, interests and approaches to the hobby differ. These differences make for lively discussions among us and give the magazine what we hope is a good mix of the articles and projects which interest most hobbyists.

In this chapter, we offer a glimpse of the diverse personalities who make up the NN staff and help give the magazine the "personal touch" which makes it distinctive.

Miniaturists need little excuse to have a party, especially when it's a lovely summer day in 1918 and the bleak days of World War I are over. This lively, colorful scene executed in 1" scale captures the best of the miniatures world in its design and craftsmanship. Its successful blend of realistic detail and good humor is a delight.

Photo by Chris Becker

Nutshell News Founding Editor Catherine B. MacLaren has been in love with dolls, dollhouses, toys and miniatures since childhood, and her approach to the hobby has retained that imaginative and inquisitive style over the years. When, at age nine, Caye received her first check for a published poem, she spent the money on miniatures.

A professional writer for many years, Caye founded Nutshell News in 1971, thus bringing the miniatures world an insightful and inspiring publication. Her wit and style infused the magazine with a distinctive flair. Caye has encouraged countless artisans, giving many of them their first national publicity through Nutshell News. Caye's Miniatours to England and her much-loved book *This Side of Yesterday* were firsts in the field.

CATHERINE B. MACLAREN
Founding Editor

Caye says she is "beguiled by antiques" both miniature and full-size, and she also collects porcelain figures, minerals, shells, dolls, books, and information. She has worked with special children, been active in children's theater — for which she has written plays still in production — and she is an avid gardener.

The mother of three daughters, Caye says her children never cared for the dollhouses she bought them, but her grandchildren show more interest. Describing miniatures as "progressive education," Caye says, "What other hobby offers so many stimulating facets to explore at price levels from free to a fortune? And what other hobby has been around for as many centuries? Because of miniatures, I am still delving, seeking, and learning."

While I was editor of **Nutshell News**, one of my favorite covers featured a room by Alice Steele, loaned to me by Margaret Whitton, now doll curator at the Margaret Woodbury Strong Museum where some of the Steele collection is on view. I remember meeting Mrs. Steele and seeing the Tiny Old New England Museum that she created to record in miniature the small town life of New England during the last century. Her refreshing and honest approach, with children foremost, appeals to me as much now as then when we discussed our mutual love for dolls and nostalgia. That is why this setting, The Doll Shop, is one of my selections, as the dolls are the jewels, and because Mrs. Steele took this scene from a memory of her childhood.

Photo courtesy the Margaret Woodbury Strong Museum

Each time I look at the photograph of Herb Randle's oil painting of Ann Meehan, I see something new. The setting was suggested by a photo of the late collector Marianne Wilson which appeared in the now out of print book **This Side of Yesterday.** Ms. Wilson told me that on her demise she wanted her collection sold at auction; how relieved I was to spot some of her things in this picture! Seeing Ann's smile I recall how she held two full-time jobs to sustain her hobby and how she had a dollhouse too large to fit through her front door hoisted to an upper floor with a larger window. Here Ann suggests a princess doing her needlework while surrounded by her loyal subjects. Those same hands have known split nails from dollhouse restorations and have taken countless notes on research. The colors and composition of the picture seem to combine the concept of the past and present for miniature posterity.

Photo and painting by Herb Randle

Having enjoyed an early version of Maynard Manor first in a brochure and later in person, I read every word about this 42-room castle in the **Nutshell News** series (August 1980 — November 1982). To me, the Manor pleases the senses and has just the right touch of nonsense thanks to its proprietors, John and Ellen Blauer, who have combined the best of their individual talents with the best of other contemporary artisans and melded into the project many priceless items from fabulous collections from the past. I agonized over which picture from the series to choose! Sir Malcolm's Withdrawing Room somehow titillated me most. Amusing and beautifully put together, it incorporates pieces from such choice collections as those amassed by Mother Larke and Jack Norworth with work by contemporary artisans such as Emily Good, Wilma Anderson, Eric Pearson and the late and beloved Susan Hendrix. Sir Malcolm was made by Vicki Newhouse, and Lady Agatha, kiln cousin to a doll I cherish, was created by Martha Farnsworth. This room is a classic example to me of the three Cs of miniaturing: Collecting, contriving and creating.

Photo by Ellen Blauer

9

DEE SNYDER
Associate Editor

Dee Snyder wrote her first book at age 14 — an illustrated children's book which was reviewed in *The New York Times*. She went on to receive a degree in journalism from Ohio University and has contributed many articles to hobby and craft magazines over the years.

A miniatures collector since her youth and a crafter by preference, Dee combines her interests, talents and training as Associate Editor of Nutshell News. She contributed to Caye MacLaren's book, *This Side of Yesterday*, writes the NN column "The Collectables" and other features, designed the Nutshell News Plans Service book *Stable of Champions*, and authored *The ABCs of Baker Street*, a miniature book on Sherlock Holmes. Dee is an avid Sherlockian and member of the Baker Street Irregulars.

A certified interior designer, Dee feels full-size decorating trends are often mirrored in the miniatures world. Her personal tastes run toward the country look, both in miniature and her full-size home with its stable where Dee displays her collection and maintains her private workshop. She has transferred her full-size ceramics and oil painting skills to miniature, offering a complete line of country accessories under the business name The Stable.

When Dee is not busy with miniatures, she is mother to two grown sons, three Italian greyhounds, a flock of guinea hens, and a pumpkin patch. She and her husband have traveled extensively in the US and abroad, where Dee enjoys seeking out regional folk toys. In addition to miniatures, Dee collects children's books, miniature books, antique toys, and all things Sherlockian.

Photo courtesy Mary Penet & Phil Levigne

I *was enchanted by this 1" interpretation of Michael Hague's illustration for* **Wind in the Willows** *before it appeared in the April 1983 issue. Kenneth Grahame's classic story of life on an English riverbank is one of my favorites. Talented miniature-making couple Mary Penet and Phil Levigne have captured the dark, cozy atmosphere of the kind Badger's kitchen where Mole, Ratty and Toad are surrounded by a rich stash of winter food supplies. This room appeals not only because of its subject and because Mary and Phil have recreated it with such skill and taste, but also for sentimental reasons. I first encountered this cast of characters while standing in a college bookstore waiting for my husband of a few months. I passed my enthusiasm for the book on to my mother and eventually to my sons — we still quote the book. I have often thought of miniaturizing a scene from it, but am now satisfied to enjoy this splendid version.*

Before reading about miniaturist Doug Friedlander's theater design background, I sensed it in his Laurel Towne Curio Shop exterior. The setting is full of the theatrical magic, artistic know-how, and creative contriving which I love. He uses proscenium effects, false perspective and dramatic lighting. This and the other buildings in his six-foot long miniature village are washed with rosy glazes to give the glow of sunset. The picture embodies much that I enjoy about miniature designing — the fantasy or storybook ambiance, use of rhythm to capture the viewer's eye, and the challenge of being original in an era of sameness made possible by manufactured components, kits, how-to's, and even identical "found objects." This scene is supposedly set in New Orleans, but to me it is like a medieval German fairy tale setting — appropriate since Doug gained his theatrical experience while serving in the US military in Germany.

Photo by Doug Kennedy

This November 1982 cover picture is a whimsical study in contrasts. All this elegance in a pumpkin amused me. The mixture of scales, textures, and rich dark colors with lighter shades is visually exciting. The pumpkin's interior was executed by Susan Sirkis in 1/2" scale. Susan was designing and working comfortably in a variety of scales before the resurgence, or even the defining, of 1/2" scale. I first met Susan in the pages of the now out of print **Toy Trader** magazine. When we met about a dozen years ago, our first conversation was about Susan doing a **Nutshell News** article on building a small scale Victorian house. The project was published in 1974, and Susan is still coming up with fresh ideas for the magazine, like this pumpkin that could be the ruffled prison of Peter Pumpkin-Eater's wife, or another concoction of Cinderella's fairy godmother.

Photo by Marty Potter

ANN RUBLE
Editor & Associate Publisher

Although she had a dollhouse as a child, Ann Ruble was not a miniaturist when she joined the staff of Nutshell News as Managing Editor in 1978. But the exquisite craftsmanship and genuine enthusiasm she found among hobbyists quickly transformed her. Starting with a collection of porcelain and ceramic pieces, she has progressed to tiny houses of all kinds, dolls — particularly Pierrot figures — and all manner of country furnishings and accessories.

Four years spent absorbing the atmosphere of Colonial Williamsburg while attending the College of William and Mary reinforced Ann's love for buildings and historic preservation. This, plus a stint with an architecture magazine, made the transition to Nutshell News a natural one. During her tenure with NN, she has made many notable changes including a switch from a quarterly to monthly format. Along with the staff, she strives to present the most interesting material and professionally executed photographs. In an effort to promote miniatures, she has acted as a spokesperson for the hobby through speaking engagements and work with the national media.

Ann says she has been greatly impressed by the miniatures world — the talent, artistry, knowledge and friendliness its hobbyists exude. "The miniatures world," she observes, "is a complete slice of life where all things are possible. Miniatures let us escape to a place where we can dream larger-than-life dreams and make them happen." Miniaturing is often fondly described by hobbyists as an "addiction." To this description Ann adds, "Miniatures are the most pleasant and educational of vices."

Tales of romance, beautiful princesses, shimmering castles — these are the inspirations from which numerous miniature settings spring. Britain's Princess Diana is a modern-day embodiment of all things romantic. As the royal couple's family grows, it is particularly fitting that doll artist Susan Sirkis chose to execute this touching portrait of the drowsy mother-to-be for the 1983 NAME National Houseparty theme "Lullaby Time In Nanny's Nursery." I am an admirer of the Princess and of Susan Sirkis, whose skills in doll making and costume design are well known to miniaturists. Susan is a friend, wise counsel and invaluable resource to me, and this doll reminds me of the friendship and fondness for romance which we share.

The cover of our June 1983 issue on the country look in miniature is a favorite among the many rooms settings our staff has assembled over the years. This room, envisioned as the home of a New England collector and antiques dealer, encompasses the essence of the country look of which I am particulary fond. Gathering items for this room from some of the best contemporary artisans working in country and primitive styles was a delight, and assembling them into a cozy setting was a joy. This is a room I could live in, basking in the afternoon sun as I read a book. It is a peaceful, inviting setting filled with the things I love.

Photo by Don Stegall

Despite a love for ''the country look'' in decorating, I occasionally get the urge to pamper myself in the elegance of a Victorian setting. California artisan Garnet Lichtenhan specializes in fashioning all silk upholstery for fine furniture. Her work suits my taste for Victorian furniture because it is rich and elegant without being gaudy. This photo, taken by **Nutshell News** contributor Anne Smith, is also significant as a reminder of the personal and professional bond which has developed over the years between Anne and myself.

Photo by Anne D. Smith

Sybil Harp has enjoyed a long career in crafts and miniatures, as founding editor of Creative Crafts (1967) and The Miniature Magazine (1976), both published by Carstens Publications. Sybil moved from the editorial side of publishing to business and advertising when she joined Nutshell News in 1979. Her successful relationship with industry leaders and NN advertisers has contributed to the magazine's success.

Sybil's husband is a model railroading buff and dollhouse builder who shares her interest in small scale objects. A predilection for teddy bears and rabbit bells characterizes Sybil's own collecting

SYBIL HARP
Associate Publisher (Business)

interest. She enjoys attending miniatures shows and meeting the people involved in the hobby. "I love seeing the new ideas they constantly come up with," she says, "and I enjoy their enthusiasm for all aspects of the world of miniatures."

Her major interest outside miniatures is her family: four children, three children-in-law, and a new grandchild. A nature lover who has turned her backyard into a wildlife sanctuary, Sybil also enjoys reading books on philosophy, psychology, and religion — subjects which, she says, "many people probably consider pretty dry stuff!"

Photo by Charles Claudon

Ruby's Christmas *by Charles Claudon was first displayed at the 1980 NAME National Houseparty in Washington, DC. The word "poignant" has been used to describe this scene and indeed it evoked an immediate, strong emotional response from me. I* **know** *Ruby — the kind of person she is, the sort of life she lives, and even some facts about her past. Hers is a solitary life but not a lonely one. She is not wealthy, but neither is she poor. Her apartment is filled with worn, comfortable furniture and is decorated with items of sentimental value. Ruby leads a quiet life, enjoying the companionship of her cats, an occasional visit from her children and grandchildren, and many happy memories of earlier years. Not only do I feel I know Ruby, but I also enjoy, in contemplating this picture, a sense of peace and contentment.*

❧ PERSONAL FAVORITES ❧

Helen Ruthberg's February 1982 article, "Love is..." presented five miniature settings containing accessories connoting "love." One of these, "The Artist's Studio," is a favorite of mine, partly because I find the scene lighthearted in spirit and fascinating in detail, but largely because it was created by an old friend. Pictures on the studio walls (including the modernistic "Love" hanging over the bed) were painted by Helen, who is a superior artist in any scale. Her work is uniquely her own, and always done primarily for the joy of it. More than any other, I think this room expresses Helen's fun-filled approach to miniatures, and for me it serves as a memento of the person who gave me my first glimpse into the world of miniatures.

Photo by Helen Ruthberg

I photographed "Herman Melville's Study at Arrowhead," a miniature room by the Berkshire and Lenox, MA garden clubs, while covering Miniatures at The Mount, a miniatures show held at author Edith Wharton's magnificent Georgian mansion in Lenox, MA. While in the Berkshires during a glorious October weekend, I visited Arrowhead and saw the study where Herman Melville wrote **Moby Dick**, one of my favorite books. Later that weekend I was elated to find the miniature version in The Mount exhibit. The room appeared exact in every detail, even to the view through the window showing the humpbacked mountain that became a great white whale in Melville's imagination. For me this photo serves as a souvenir of a memorable weekend highlighted by miniatures with a literary flavor.

❧ PERSONAL FAVORITES ❧

BONNIE SCHROEDER
Managing Editor

Since she joined the NN staff with the April 1981 issue, Bonnie Schroeder has come to love the miniatures hobby and the people involved in it. Coming from a crafts background, she enjoys do-it-yourself projects, but also admires and purchases work by artisans. Bonnie has made break-away boxes, nurseries, a linen shop, Victorian country kitchen, general store, barber shop and a mechanic's garage as gifts for friends and family. Bonnie has the enviable talent of being able to put a few odds and ends together and make a finished setting — a skill which comes in handy when assembling rooms for NN photos.

Bonnie is married with one son, two dachshunds, one chihuahua, and one dachsyhuahua. She has collected owls, antique Victorian furniture and pink Depression glass for about 15 years, often spending weekends at auctions, flea markets and yard sales searching for new "treasures." She says NN has become a focal point in her career and her life. As she advanced from Assistant Editor to Managing Editor to Editor (effective with the September 1984 issue), Bonnie's knowledge of miniatures, interior decorating and period furnishings, arts, crafts, etc. has also grown. "Working in this field," she says, "expands your knowledge in all aspects of living, past and present."

At the 1983 Ashland, VA "Back To College" miniatures weekend, doll maker Susan Sirkis exhibited one of the most beautiful dolls I've ever encountered. A little larger than 1" scale, this voluptuous lady is one of the so-called "Naughtie Nudies" made in the 1920s. The features on this doll are so realistic, it's hard to believe she isn't a real person. I'm a great admirer of Susan's work, and the gown she created for the doll's owner Marjorie Brandt is the perfect accent to this exquisite figure. Mel Prescott, a long-time artisan in the miniatures field, made the chaise on which this lady casually reclines.

Owls are my passion. For the past 15 years I've collected owls in every shape and size — from ceramic and wood to porcelain, pewter and anything else I've found. When I began collecting miniatures five years ago, I also started collecting miniature owls. During this time, I developed another passion — Mary McGrath's sculptures. While traveling to shows and photographing artisans' pieces for **Nutshell News**, I learned that no matter how close the camera's eye got to one of Mary's nature figures, the detail was perfect. My two passions came together when I photographed Mary's snowy white owl at the 1982 IGMA show.

When we were preparing the March 1983 issue on teddy bears, tiny bears, bears, and more bears arrived in our offices daily, and the entire staff became immersed in bearophilia, bearobilia and bearbliography. Among these bears, one group stood out for their life-like qualities and individualism — the TiggyWinkles bears made by Kathryn Franze and Susan Johnson. I immediately fell in love with these little characters who portray every role in life from beararinas to bear brides.

Photo by Elizabeth Ellsworth

❧ PERSONAL FAVORITES ❧

BONNIE BENNETT
Special Projects Editor

Bonnie Bennett was already a talented miniaturist when she joined the Nutshell News staff in January 1982. Now she is also a diversified craftsperson. As Special Projects Editor, Bonnie test builds all the how-to projects in NN from needlework to electrification, including kits for the Product Review column and projects for The Nutshell News Plans Service. She also builds rooms, houses, and "sets" which act as backdrops for the magazine's cover photos.

Bonnie has served as president of two Virginia miniatures clubs since her introduction to the hobby in 1976 when she began a dollhouse for her daughter. She has also donated her time and talents to making favors for the Virginia Miniature Enthusiasts "Back To College" miniatures gathering.

A native Virginian and a direct descendant of Benjamin Harrison, a signer of the Declaration of Independence, Bonnie is also a history buff — particularly Virginia history —and hopes to one day build a miniature version of Brandon, her ancestors' James River plantation.

Bonnie says she inherited her crafting aptitude from her creative mother and artist father. Her father, Marshall Harrison, a retired professional model shipbuilder for the Newport News Shipyard, has joined Bonnie in miniature crafting as a fine furniture builder. Bonnie says his 23 years of model making experience come in handy when she needs advice.

Most of Bonnie's time is taken up with Nutshell News projects, designing and building a line of nursery furniture and toys for her own small miniatures business, and running an active household made up of a 13-year-old son and a 10-year-old daughter. Bonnie's collecting interests center on larger dolls from around the world and 1″ scale toys and pottery. In spare moments, she likes to get away from it all by hiking in the Virginia mountains.

*Fascination with Britain's Royal Family inspired artisan Brooke Tucker to create Prince William's nursery in 1″ scale. Things came together so easily that Brooke feels she was destined to create this nursery based on an artist's rendering of the full-size room featured in **Ladies Home Journal**. Brooke's good eye for detail and ingenuity can be seen throughout the room. Nurseries captivate me, and Prince William's delightful room is no exception. Brooke has achieved striking similarity to the drawing through her use of colors, furniture and accessories she built for this charming room.*

Throughout her Holly Hobbie dollhouse, **Nutshell News** Associate Editor Dee Snyder uses many of her American primitive miniatures to create a contemporary decor. My favorite room in the house is the cozy pink child's room. Combining delicate roses with gingham, quilts and farm animals, Dee has successfully styled a feminine and romantic country bedroom. Most of the furnishings were collected from other craftspeople, but Dee crafted some items herself. She upholstered the sofa using her own silk-screened quilts, and the horse collection she created is evidence of her love for horses. Lambs and teddy bears also abound. Toys are among my favorite miniatures so it is easy to understand why I like this room. I also admire the way Dee has created a charming American provincial scene by tastefully combining prints, colors and fabrics with her country collection.

Photo by Dee Snyder

Arlyn Coad is not only a professional puppeteer but also a miniaturist and doll artist. To create her mostly one-of-a-kind wax figures, Arlyn first sculpts in clay, then makes a plaster cast of the doll's head, hands, legs and sometimes the entire body. Once the wax is removed from the cast, the final sculpting and refinements are completed. The fine detail and realism in Arlyn's boy figure fascinate me. His intense expression exemplifies a child's inquisitive nature. The unkept appearance and hands-in-pockets stance add more character to this slightly mischievous youth who, like my own son, may have a frog, snake or unidentified creature in his pocket.

Photo courtesy Arlyn Coad

A Little House
To Call Home

Clothing, food, and shelter — three basic elements necessary for human survival. Ever since *homo erectus* and his family first huddled together in the refuge of their cave, man has found comfort and safety in his home.

Initially, home was little more than a shelter from predators and the elements. It gradually evolved into a fortress from enemies, and man's home literally became his castle. Eventually, the size and semblance of a home indicated the owner's wealth, power and social position. Today, we have more choices in the type of house we come home to than ever before. Single family detached homes, restorations, apartments, condominiums, group houses, co-ops, townhouses — the options (and prices) are staggering, and they have greatly influenced the way we live.

But regardless of the cost, shape, size or location of a home, the philosophical interpretations of this simple word — and the memories we attach to it — are intense.

When I was young, my parents and I spent many vacations peering into other people's homes. My mother drank in the rich history of the restorations in Colonial Williamsburg, Old Salem, Sturbridge Village, the plantations along Virginia's historic James River, Monticello, Mount Vernon, and many more. So avid was her interest and so frequent were our trips that my father, our grudging chauffeur, once commented, "If you've seen one old house, you've seen them all."

But for someone like my mother — who passed her love for old homes and history on to me — the past comes alive when you step over the threshold of an old home. You feel as if you could touch and speak to the former inhabitants whose portraits line the walls.

The same is true for miniaturists when they peer inside a dollhouse, because the house transports them to another place and time. Dollhouses are wonderful documentaries of daily life. This is why a miniaturist who collects antiques is thrilled by the discovery of a house with its original furniture, or a house which has remained in the same family for several generations. Through such houses, the viewer can glean immense insight into the lives of the children who played with the house and the social mores and daily preoccupations of the adults who built it.

Despite the haunting charm of these antique houses, the majority of today's miniaturists prefer to build, kit bash, or buy homes which fit their specifications. These houses and their furnishings act as documents of history in two ways: They preserve the period they replicate, and they also shed light on the era in which they were built.

Many miniaturists chose to duplicate a house which occupies a nostalgic place in their memory, even if the house isn't old enough to qualify for the National Register of Historic Places. These are often reproductions of childhood homes, a home the miniaturist currently occupies, or a dream dwelling. Whatever style of architecture you chose to duplicate in miniature, you are preserving a building you love, a building made beautiful by its pillars and beams and by the memories, dreams, and hopes it holds. The miniaturist who reproduces a home from the past preserves history. The miniaturist who builds a contemporary home or a dream house makes history by documenting daily life for future generations.

There is a vast difference between a house and a home. "Home is where the heart is," and any miniaturist who has toiled for hours applying individual fishscale shingles, or worried over plumb walls, or cursed brick corner joints will tell you that a good amount of love went into that miniature dwelling. Quite often, the home was built for a loved one, for a charity, or as a showcase of the builder's talents. No matter for what reason the house came into the world, as poet Edgar Guest explained it, "Ye've got to love each brick an' stone from cellar up t' dome: It takes a heap o' livin' in a house t' make it home."

There was an old dame called Tartine
Had a house made of butter and cream;
Its walls were of flour, it is said,
And its floors were of gingerbread!

—French Nursery Rhyme

Jackie Barlow has been a collector and dealer in antiques, both full-size and miniature, for many years. Growing up near Cape May, NJ, Jackie has come to love the colorful, restored Victorian homes in this seaside resort. When she needed a dollhouse for her growing collection of contemporary miniatures, Jackie commissioned Charles Bates to construct this 15-room White House which evokes the mood of Cape May's grand old homes. The glass-roofed solarium is a graceful addition to the turreted facade with its mansard roof and widow's walk. Inside, a spiral staircase is the focal point of the entrance hall.

Photo courtesy Jackie Barlow

*How would you like to take with
you your house upon your back,
And such a funny house as this —
all curly, brown, and black?*

—Lucy Diamond, The Snail

Thomas Latane built his first dollhouse when he was in high school, and he has made his living as a miniatures craftsperson ever since. This Georgian mansion with 12 dormers, 26 columns, 2 glass-enclosed porches, and a carport is a 1'' scale replica of a Baltimore, MD mansion Tom built for the full-size home's owners. Tom prefers to carve his own stair rails, fireplaces, and moldings.

Photo courtesy Thomas Latane

Miniature preservationists Ken and Miriam Schaefer and Bob and Ginny Schmitz built this 3/4'' scale replica of a ca. 1878 Italianate Victorian saved by the Kirkwood, MO, Historical Society. Steve Saller, who commissioned the 13-room replica for his wife Lisl, grew up in the full-size home.

Photo by Bob Schmitz

The Wenham Museum in Wenham, MA boasts a fine collection of 19th century games, toys, and dollhouses, including the ca. 1884 Chamberlain House described by dollhouse historian Flora Gill Jacobs in her book **A History of Dolls' Houses** as representing the ultimate in Victoriana. The eight-room house was built by Salem, MA silversmith Benjamin Chamberlain for his two daughters and includes a silver tea service and a family of dolls dressed in their original clothes.

O, to have a little house!
To own the hearth and stool and all!

—Padraic Colum, An Old Woman of the Roads

A teacher and librarian by trade, Tom Buchta says his free-time interest is in architecture and interior design. He began custom designing dollhouses in 1975 and now works with his clients much as an architect would, supplying them with floor plans and preliminary sketches. He builds in many styles from Victorians and brownstones to the wood and glass multi-angle contemporary shown here.

The Atlanta Toy Museum is a magical place which infects both children and adult visitors with the joy of collecting and enjoying antique toys, dolls, and dollhouses. This ornate, ca. 1870 French Bird Cage house was probably once used as a home for stuffed perfume birds.

Photo by Kern Thompson

Mother Goose had a house,
'T was built in a wood,
An owl at the door
For a porter stood

This Victorian dollhouse built by Harleen Alexander aptly fits the saying, ``A man's home is his castle.'' Photographed in the Victorian Gardens overlooking the Smithsonian Institution's Castle building, the nine-room house features four fireplaces with handcarved mantels, double porches, and a copper-roofed tower room off the master bedroom. Harleen has long been fascinated with architecture, and through her travels as an Air Force pilot's wife, she has been exposed to many regional building styles. She incorporates these regional touches in the four to five miniature homes she builds yearly.

Photo by Olive Rosen

When I have a house . . .
as I sometimes may . . .
I'll suit my fancy in every way

—Don Blanding, Vagabond House

In a miniatures world which grows more sophisticated each year, it is refreshing to know that some people still enjoy creating works of art from cardboard, glue and string. Lola Dube, a painter and doll maker born in Austria during the last century, built this exquisite Victorian from odds and ends kept in the top drawer of a desk which serves as her work table.

For 25 years, Richard Tucker built full-size wooden mockups of space stations and astronaut shuttle trainers for Rockwell International. Now he applies his building skills to 1'' scale dollhouses like this Queen Anne tower house constructed for his wife Nancy. The house measures 25''W x 42''D x 50''H and boasts a glowing, natural wood finish.

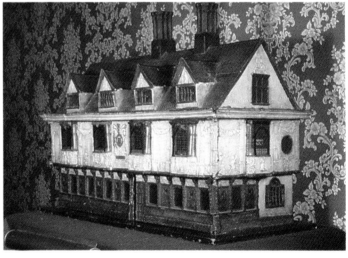

The Silver Jubilee Dolls' House Gallery in Fort Erie, Ontario, is said to be the world's largest private dollhouse collection, representing 30 years of collecting by founder Mildred M. Mahoney. The museum's 120 fully furnished miniature homes date from the 18th century on and include the Ancient House of Ipswich shown here. Considered the keystone house in the collection, it was built 70 years ago and was sent to Boston in 1977 as a tribute to Queen Elizabeth's Silver Jubilee Year. The house is a replica of a 400-year-old house used by English king Charles II as a hiding place during the Cromwellian uprisings.

Magical Landscapes

In Lewis Carroll's *Alice In Wonderland*, his small heroine was enchanted by a glimpse of a lovely garden. Wishing to walk through the tiny door into this peaceful place, Alice drank a magic potion which made her shrink enough to fit through the entrance. Unfortunately, circumstances kept Alice from enjoying that lovely spot.

A miniaturist doesn't need a potion to create a magical landscape. With a little ingenuity, the hobbyist can create anything from a formal English garden to a lush tropical paradise.

Like many aspects of miniaturing, landscaping in scale is not new. No doubt a pharoah's tomb held a replica of servants tending a garden to assure the ruler's nutrition in the After Life. Many turn of the century dollhouses have fenced yards and flower-filled window boxes.

In a contemporary miniature setting, use of plants as part of a room's decor offers a finishing touch and a heightened sense of realism. These decorative elements subtley suggest a human presence: A house or room with thriving plants is surely the home of a caring individual.

The language of flowers can also help set the tone of a room. Hanging plants, potted trees and succulents suggest a casual, contemporary look. Large ferns and dried arrangements under domes or pressed into pictures lend a Victorian feeling. Williamsburg-style arrangements of fruits and flowers indicate a more formal atmosphere.

Outside the dollhouse, trees, rose trellises, boxwood hedges, brick walkways, or urns of geraniums transform a pretty house into an inviting home.

Commercial products designed for miniature landscaping are readily available. Some have been designed specifically with dollhouses in mind. Others have been used by model railroaders for years. In fact, these hobbyists pride themselves on the sophistication of their landscaped train layouts, and rightly so. Their skill in using a variety of craft materials to create realistic scenery is noteworthy. Miniaturists interested in developing their green thumb would do well to study the landscaping books written by model railroaders. Some landscaping kits are also available for the first-timer.

Hobbyists interested in making plants and flowers for dollhouses have a wide variety of materials to choose from. Miniature greenery has been successfully cultivated from such materials as bread dough, Sculpey, Fimo, florist tape and wire, crepe, tissue, tracing and quilling papers, seeds, shells and other marine life, beads, silk and other delicate fabrics, ribbons and trims, shredded foam, even metal. Real flowers and plants in either living or dried form are also possibilities.

The use of living plants in miniature settings has been honed to a fine art by participants in the annual *Philadelphia Flower Show*. Since 1975, this event has featured a special category for miniature rooms incorporating living plants. Participants exhibiting miniature rooms must adhere to detailed requirements set by the Philadelphia Horticulture Society. Horticulture must be featured and only live or dried plant materials are permitted. Exhibits must be kept in good condition throughout the eight-day show, which means that plants must be watered regularly and pruned if necessary. Assuring easy access to the plants often tests a miniaturist's design and building skills. The creator's manual dexterity can also be sorely tried when maneuvering a watering can beneath floors or around walls without destroying the setting.

Your approach can be as formal or whimsical as you desire. Entries in the 1981 and 1982 AMSI Miniatures landscaping contests varied from Victorian flower gardens to modern patios to backyard vegetable gardens to an enchanted forest inhabited by sprites.

Think of your garden as a retreat, and decide what you would enjoy most in such a special place. I would want lilies of the valley, honeysuckle, and lilacs in my garden — what a riot of scents that would be! A moss-covered cliff would overlook the sea, and ferns would shelter a secret pool. Impossible that such diverse vegetation should exist in one spot, you say? Not in my magical, miniature garden!

Under the window is my garden,
Where sweet, sweet flowers grow;
And in the pear tree dwells a robin,
The dearest bird I know

—Kate Greenaway

Miniature landscape artist Maggie Bock comes from a family of professional gardeners, so a historical and botanical knowledge of plants comes naturally to her. Maggie uses only natural plant materials — many of them exotic and difficult to obtain — and prepares them for 1" scale landscapes using a four-part process of drying, bleaching, dyeing and softening. This Victorian garden took first place in the dealer category in the 1981 AMSI Miniature Landscaping Contest.

Photo by M. Elaine Adams

*Flowers are words
which even a babe may understand*

—Bishop Coxe, The Singing of Birds

The language of flowers is universal, even in miniature, and these tiny arrangements can add graceful charm and beautiful color to your miniature rooms. Delicately crafted plants and flowers heighten the sense of realism in a miniature setting and breathe life into an otherwise static environment.

Mexican artist Alicia Cuadra uses an old family bread dough recipe to make the flowers shown here. Once the flowers are formed, she "porcelainizes" them to prevent crumbling.

Mary Payne began her miniatures career using bread dough to make her flowers and plants. Over the years she has experimented with other media, including crepe paper. These arrangements combine the two materials for vibrant effects.

Miniature flowers come in all varieties and are made from numerous craft materials. In the late 1970s, Floridian Helene Krupick scaled down her full-size shell flower business to design 1" scale arrangements like the ones, at right, from tiny shells and non-producing marine life.

Shed no tear! O, shed no tear!
The flower will bloom another year

—John Keats, Fairy Song

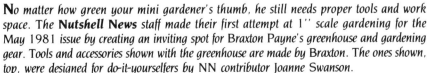

No matter how green your mini gardener's thumb, he still needs proper tools and work space. The **Nutshell News** staff made their first attempt at 1'' scale gardening for the May 1981 issue by creating an inviting spot for Braxton Payne's greenhouse and gardening gear. Tools and accessories shown with the greenhouse are made by Braxton. The ones shown, top, were designed for do-it-yourselfers by NN contributor Joanne Swanson.

The Victorians adored all things ornamental, elaborate and colorful. In this era, ladies of privilege pursued such genteel hobbies as making dried flower arrangements. Bucharest-born Otilia Levy, a gardener and painter, creates what she calls "floral fantasies" in miniature using the tiniest flowers from her extensive garden. After her flowers are dried, Otilia assembles them under domes, pressed in pictures, or in tiny flower-decoupaged boxes.

A *garden is a lovesome thing*

—Thomas Edward Brown, My Garden

David Krupick, formerly in the drapery and interior design business, was cajoled into miniature making by his mother, miniaturist Helene Krupick. Since the early 1970s, David has made a mark for himself in the miniatures world by building distinctive gazebos, garden rooms and lawn furniture. This gazebo, inspired by an existing structure in New Orleans, LA, was the first piece designed for **The Nutshell News Plans Service** in 1981.

Rooms executed by F.H. ``Ham'' and Cerina Gouge are always favorites when they are displayed in the Philadelphia area. The Gouges' gentle touches of humor and nostalgia make their settings, like this ca. 1900 Fourth of July picnic, a joy to view. This scene, which incorporates living plants and a painted backdrop, was an entry in the 1980 Philadelphia Flower Show.

Photo by Dareus Conover

Hie to haunts right seldom seen,
Lovely, lonesome, cool, and green!
Over bank and over brae,
Hie away, hie away!

—Sir Walter Scott, Hie Away, Hie Away

Hanging baskets, potted plants, climbing vines, a shady tree — landscaping adds the finishing touch to any outdoor setting. Virginia Greene built this relaxing scene typical of many backyards in Marin County, CA, near where she lives and works on miniatures. Virginia built the hot tub, deck, latticework, and fence from basswood stained to resemble redwood, then finished the scene using AMSI landscaping products. The hot tub has an aquarium pump to create bubbles and tiny interior lights for nighttime bathing.

31

O how glad I am I've found you,
With Forget-me-nots around you

—Cicely Mary Barker, Forget-me-not

To create the lacy look of her one-of-a-kind wicker furniture pieces, Iphegenia Rose uses beads, string, gessoed quilling paper, wrapped wire and other materials. The shell flowers and plants shown are made by Wilma Thomas, Helene Krupick's sister who also uses marine materials in her arrangements.

The annual Philadelphia Flower Show is known for its breathtaking floral displays, long lines, and a consistently high-caliber exhibit of miniature rooms incorporating living plants. The scene shown here captured a Blue Ribbon at the 1980 Flower Show in the Miniature Room category. Miniaturist Dusty Boynton built and landscaped the scene, entitled "Sunday — A Time For Renewal". The backyard patio setting depicts a lazy Sunday morning spent enjoying a cup of coffee and the newspaper. The hammock hung in the tree-shaded niche at right is especially inviting.

Photo by Dareus Conover

A *window box of wallflowers*
Is *a garden for a king*
—Eleanor Farjeon, Window Boxes

"**M**iniatures are a way of recreating memories without spending a lot of money," says Bob Porter, author of the miniatures craft book **Building with Bob**. He and his wife Jean share a love for the Arizona desert and the handcrafts made on the state's Indian reservations. To recapture the region's beauty, the Porters built and furnished the Sonoran Desert Indian Shop. To enhance the Southwestern feeling he and Jean enjoy, Bob landscaped the shop with living cacti and gravel from the Arizona desert.

Photo by Shelby Harris

The translucence of her bread dough flowers is Michigan artisan Marcy Fischer's trademark. Working from fresh blossoms, Marcy measures the flower parts and traces petal shapes and overall structure, then copies every feature, even though some parts of the finished bloom may not be visible. Marcy's husband Perry makes 1" scale versions of antique furniture.

Rosemary Dyke came to miniatures in 1976 after many happy years in other crafts. She specializes in plants and flowers made primarily from tracing paper. She paints the various paper parts of each plant, then assembles the pieces into individual blossoms and finally into complete arrangements. Miniatures hold her interest, she says, because they encompass such variety.

In The Workplace

When I was growing up, my grandfather and father were partners in a grocery or general store. I have fond memories of visiting my grandfather there at lunch time. He would take me behind the meat counter and set me on a wooden crate while he cut fresh slices of bologna and cheese for sandwiches which I washed down with either grape or chocolate soda pop. On hot days I loved to stand in front of the meat freezer whenever it was opened, and sneak candy bars from the ice chest at the front of the store.

Years later, I still remember the place vividly: the smell of saw dust and old floor boards, the rich, bitter aroma of freshly ground coffee, the smooth green crispness of bananas pulled right from their excelsior-packed crates, the hollow metallic sound of the screen door as it banged, and the customers — mostly country people dressed in dust-covered work clothes.

No doubt many of us have similar recollections of a favorite neighborhood store where our families bought groceries and traded community news, places where we first understood the vital importance of money — at the candy counter.

The general store is one of the most common settings built and furnished by miniaturists, especially collectors new to the hobby. Beyond its sentimental appeal, the general store has other features which make it an ideal project for a beginning miniaturist.

From a construction standpoint, a general store is usually a simple frame structure with little interior or exterior ornamentation — a good start for the beginning carpenter. What might be considered "errors" in more sophisticated settings simply add flavor and character to a general store. A few warped floorboards and an uneven paint job here and there are completely acceptable, even desired.

Concern with period authenticity is often minimal, because any good general store has never been cleaned out since its doors were first opened. It therefore contains a hodgepodge of goods accumulated over time. Furnishings and decoration are haphazard, at best. The miniaturist's biggest challenge is creating a realistic look of disarray. Most of us accomplish this by filling the place with as much "stuff" as it will hold — which is perhaps the ultimate draw of the general store: It justifies our collecting frenzy. It gives the collector an excuse to buy miniatures in a wide range of categories with the secure knowledge that almost *anything* is appropriate in a general store.

License to collect a large number of miniatures, whether they be unrelated items or pieces in a specific category, the element of nostalgia, and the fact that our daily existence revolves around work in the home, office or shop, make places of business one of the miniature hobby's most popular themes. According to Dunn and Bradstreet, over 37,000 retail businesses opened in the United States in 1983. The variety of goods and services offered in these places of business is astounding and gives the miniaturist an incredible amount of creative fodder to fire his or her hobby projects. General stores, ladies' boutiques — millinery shops in particular — and medical and dental offices rank high on the list of room settings most miniaturists have completed at some point in their collecting career. The realm of commercial establishments in 1" scale ranges from kite shops to New York delicatessens to the offices of a commercial airline.

Office settings are often given as gifts to working spouses or other family members. Even a non-miniaturist can appreciate a replica which so directly relates to his or her work environment. And you never can tell — such a gift may be just the thing to get that special someone involved in *your* special hobby!

Far out beyond the city's lights, away from din and roar,
The cricket chirps of summer nights beneath the country store

—Unknown, The Country Store

Photo by Anne D. Smith

Every successful shop has its name prominently displayed on an attention-getting sign. George Schlosser, a full-size artist and miniaturist, specializes in 1'' and 1/2'' commercial signs. A former retailing executive, George prefers folk art, both in his paintings and the ca. 1890 home he and his wife Ginny share in Connecticut. However, his work spans a wide spectrum of styles and was included in a dollhouse exhibit at the White House during the 1981 Christmas season.

At the turn of the century, the local drug store was a social gathering place as well as the spot to purchase just what the doctor ordered. This Victorian Drugstore was built by Marian Borneman who has collected miniatures for over 25 years. An artist and miniatures/craft shop owner, Marian brings such nostalgic charm to this setting that you can almost taste the confections from the soda fountain. Marian's husband Henry is a pharmacist, and she has outfitted the back room with a work table and lab sink, chemicals, beakers and other tools of the pharmacist's trade. This setting was displayed at the 1981 Philadelphia Flower Show.

Photo by Carol Tabas

35

When we learn to count,
Don't you see, don't you see?
Then we'll spend my dollar,
Half for her, half for me

—Amos R. Wells

At a busy intersection in New Orleans' French Quarter stands the Boutique de Parfum, a shop where the lovely proprietress (by Galia Bazylko) will mix a scent to complement your personality. The shop, designed and built by full-size potter and long-time crafts devotee Camille Strom, centers around her collections of tiny perfume bottles and beads. All the bottles are made of cut glass or crystal and have unusual stoppers. The stopper on one bottle is a hand blown glass swan. Accessories with faux finishes or 23K gold leaf embellishments complete the scene.

Photos by Jim Cook

When we learn to write,
Don't you see, don't you see?
Then I'll write to Dolly
And she'll write to me

—Amos R. Wells

The inhabitants of this ca. 1700-1725 Connecticut parlor can enjoy a peaceful spot to do their letter writing as they sit at the pilgrim desk-on-frame. The room and its contents were built by Carl Gustafson, a teacher, artist, painter, sculptor, industrial designer, model maker, full-size builder, and miniaturist. This was Carl's first 1'' scale room.

Before the advent of ready-to-wear clothing, the tailor's or dressmaker's shop was a place of frantic activity. This shop is owned by Frank Hanley and Jeffery Gueno whose collecting centers around antiques, specifically 17th and 18th century creche figures. Frank, a classical musician, and Jeffery, an interior designer, are also gardeners, painters and collectors of rare sea shells, antique fabrics, trims and papers, and full-size Empire furniture which fills their Louisiana home. In their miniatures, the two skillfully combine rare antique finds with their own craftsmanship, giving their settings a haunting Old World aura.

Everyone buys at wonderful stalls
Toys and chocolates, guns, and sweets,
Ivory pistols, and Persian shawls
—Alfred Noyes, A Song from "The Flower of Old Japan"

Jane Betz was ahead of her time in 1978 when she planned a 1" scale gallery of boutiques. Full-size builders were just starting their shopping plazas with atriums, fountains, luxury shops and gourmet food stands. Designed and built by architect Ken Schaefer and machinist Bob Schmitz, the six-foot long gallery has eight shops which blend the sophistication, charm and whimsy of Jane's personality. The gallery features a toy and miniatures shop, ice cream parlor and tea room, tobacco and news shop, an architect and contractor's office, ladies' apparel boutique, gourmet shop, antiques shop, and one empty section awaiting a tenant. For tired feet after a day of shopping, there is even a ladies' lounge.

Photo by Herb Weitman

To market, to market, to buy a fat pig,
Home again, home again, dancing a jig

—Nursery Rhyme

Bill and Joan Helton have been active in the miniatures world for over 10 years as collectors, builders and members of the San Diego, CA Miniature Crafters club. Frequent travelers, the Heltons keep their memories fresh by building 1″ scale settings reminiscent of favorite travel stops. The Maple Corner is typical of many antiques shops found along back country roads on the East Coast. San Diego collector Joanne Gooden commissioned the room from the Heltons to house some of the first pieces she began collecting 23 years ago.

The Purple Panache, a modern version of the peddler's wagon, was made by Robin and Shawn Betterly for the 1983 Tiny Treasures show in Boston, MA. The wagon, filled with purple hats, totes, tees, stickers, and other novelties, is a 1″ version of the colorful boutique wagons found in Boston's Faneuil Hall/Quincy Market shopping district. The exhibit won first prize in the scenes and shadow boxes category at the Tiny Treasures show.

Funny, how Felicia Ropps
Always handles things in shops!

—Gelett Burgess, Felicia Ropps

The general store is an inviting place where you might find anything from a Mexican sombrero to a set of spatterware dishes. This turn of the century store was built by Al and Greg Heuer for miniaturist Shirley Swensen and includes an old-fashioned post office and second floor antiques shop.

Photo by Richard Dower

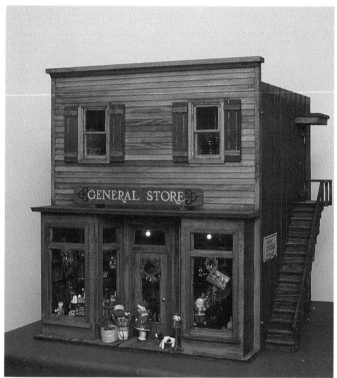

The Elizabethans loved a good festival, and the market cross building located in the town square was often the scene of such activities. When miniaturist Phyllis Zart asked her father to build a 1'' scale general store, Charles Knapp insisted she have something different: A reproduction of a ca. 1618 market cross in Norfolk, England. Mr. Knapp, a woodworking hobbyist for over 30 years, built the octagonal four-shop structure which won Best of Show and first place in the Tudor category at the 1980 Mid-Ohio Miniatures Show.

Photo by Anne D. Smith

Phelan City, a group of over 60 1'' scale buildings, was a unique concept when miniatures shop owner Roy Huntington proposed it in 1979. The town was built by a group of ''town council'' members who bought individual lots for businesses of their choice. Over 40 miniaturists from Seattle, WA to Laguna Beach, CA participated in this venture which includes several bars and restaurants, apparel and gift shops, a museum, art gallery and movie theater, sporting goods store, pet, hobby, and toy shops, a car dealership, post office, church, jail, and town hall.

I wish I lived in a caravan,
With a horse to drive like a peddler-man!
—William Brighty Rands, The Peddler's Caravan

Mickey Mouse is unlikely to discover cures for any human ills other than overt curiosity in this fantasy laboratory based on the Walt Disney tale **The Sorcerer's Apprentice**. The setting was created by Madelyn Cook for the 1979 NAME Region N-2 houseparty's ``School Days'' theme.

Photo by Jim Cook

Many a teen-aged boy has hung around the local gas station gleaning tips from seasoned mechanics on how to fix cars, play cards, and understand women. Missouri dollhouse builder Don Cole made a departure from his one-of-a-kind 1'' scale Victorian mansions and Italianate villas to design this weathered ca. 1920-30 gas station in kit form.

Photo by Judy Davis

For centuries, gypsies have conducted business from their gaily decorated wagons. This lovely gypsy lady leads a comfortable life, as her tastefully appointed wagon shows. Judee Williamson adapted this wagon from The Lawbre Company's peddler wagon kit and outfitted it with a bunk bed, cooking facilities and all the tools necessary for a lady who ``takes in a little sewing''.

Now I have apples and candy to sell,
And more nice things than I can tell

—Maud Lindsay, from ''The Little Gray Pony''

Photo by Sarah Salisbury

Not every workplace can be quiet as a library, tempting as a boutique or clean as a scientific lab. Grime, soot and dirt under the fingernails are typical in many work settings, like Iova Vaughn's 1845 blacksmith's shop. Her father and grandfather were farmer/blacksmiths, and Iova studies restored blacksmiths' shops wherever she travels. This 1'' setting includes a brick forge, leather bellows, anvil, slack tub, grindstone and smaller hand tools. Iova's expert aging gives the scene the look of many years of hard use.

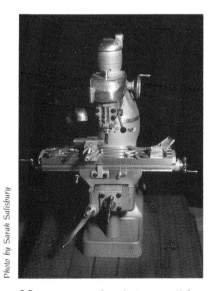

Photo by Sarah Salisbury

Miniaturists with a do-it-yourself bent are fascinated by George Apostol's working 1'' scale version of a milling machine.

Victor Root spent 14 months building his first 1'' scale project: this Woodworking Shop exhibited at the 1983 Saratoga Festival of Miniatures. The shop has 2000 individually placed floor pegs, 1500 cedar shingles, and 408 bricks in the chimney. Befitting the festival's theme ''Miniatures In Motion,'' the shop has a sophisticated electrical system in which the background scene shifts from day to night lighting.

Photo by Elizabeth Ellsworth

Chink, chink, chocket,
Pennies in my pocket!

—Mexican Rhyme

Photo by Robert F. Will

Jeff Steele has taken an artistic approach to miniatures since he was in high school over 10 years ago. Jeff views his rooms — many designed as shops — as three-dimensional artistic compositions in which angles, planes, color and texture play major roles. He designed this 16th century European workshop, Le Petit Shoppe, so the viewer first notices the interior, then gradually exits into a background filled with mysterious open doors and windows, hidden alleys and textured surfaces.

Specialty shops, particularly those focusing on ethnic or regional wares, reflect the customs and lifestyles of the people whose goods they sell. Making such a shop in miniature is an educational experience which gives the collector a specific theme for his or her purchases. Bob and Jean Porter built their Sonoran Desert Indian Shop around goods made by American Indians. Hopi kachinas, Navaho rugs, Santa Clara pottery, and Papago baskets give this shop an authentic Southwestern flavor.

There is no frigate like a book
To take us lands away

—Emily Dickinson, A Book

Many miniaturists share a love for books, especially general fiction and history titles. These hobbyists usually enjoy the research required to complete a room as much as they enjoy the construction process. In spare moments they can be found in their miniatures work area, in the library doing mini research, or curled up with a good book. Miniature book collecting itself is an active hobby supporting approximately 50 publishers and some 400 serious collectors worldwide.

Photo by Dee Snyder

This elegant ca. 1770 library holds an impressive collection — of miniatures. Mike Powell and his wife Lari collaborate on rooms like the library at Mellerstain in Scotland, above, one in a series of historic period rooms they call ''Windows on the Past''. Lari does extensive research before Mike — whose love for plaster work is evident in this room's ceiling — builds the room, furniture, accessories, moldings and trims.

Photo courtesy Mike Powell

Miniature books have a rich history dating to Gutenberg's day. It is believed that the first ''little'' book was printed in 1468 in Germany. ''Mon Plaisir'', the dollhouse project begun in 1716 by Duchess Augusta Dorothea of Schwarzburg-Gotha, also includes some printed volumes. Today's tiny tomes range from 3'' tall down to a 1.4mm copy of the Lord's Prayer printed in Tokyo, Japan and considered the most recent ''smallest book''. The group here includes old and new micro books less than 3'' tall.

Since man first took brush to paper, desks have been vital to letter writing, bill paying, the drafting and signing of laws, and general musing with pen in hand. This Federal style desk with leather top, rosewood banding and brass details was built by British cabinet-maker, antiques restorer and miniaturist John Davenport who began his miniatures career making replicas of 3'' scale apprentice pieces.

What do you sell, O ye merchants?
Richly your wares are displayed.
Turbans of crimson and silver,
Tunics of purple brocade

—Sarojini Naidu, In the Bazaars of Hyderabad

Artisans Noel and Pat Thomas were among the first craftspeople to use weathering and aging in their 1" buildings. Their Twentieth Street Emporium is reminiscent of a store Noel and his father visited on Saturdays when Noel was a boy. This three-story brick building houses a soda shop, post office and business office, second story living quarters, and a third floor artist's studio. Aged advertising signs and vestiges of a building no longer standing can be seen on the side wall.

Photo by Noel & Pat Thomas

Artist B-Lu Hugill displays her miniature silver and accessories in this replica of Tiffany's, the world-renowned jewelry and gift store. The two-story shop was built by Bill and Joan Helton. Friends of the Hugills donated old jewelry and photographed, sketched and took notes on areas of the building where full-size construction and layout information was needed. The late silversmith Guglielmo Cini made several pieces for the shop. In addition to its silver and jewels, the tiny Tiffany's features a working revolving door and a clock shaped like Atlas supporting the world on the building's exterior.

Photo by Bob Van Doren

If a library is judged by the quality of its books, this 1" high volume alone would have patrons clamoring to enter the library doors. This handpainted, leather-bound **Book of Hours** was printed by miniature book publisher Barbara Raheb of Collector Editions.

45

*There was a rustling that seemed like a bustling
Of merry crowds justling at pitching and hustling*

—Robert Browning, The Pied Piper of Hamelin

This busy Main Street could be in your home town, but it is situated on four acres of lovely English countryside in the Torbay section of Southwest England. Babbacombe Village is the second of two miniature towns built by T.F. Dobbins. The 1'' scale town includes 250 model buildings, hundreds of figures individually carved by Mr. Dobbins, 1000 feet of model railway, and such whimsically named businesses as Ann Teak Furniture Co. and A. McAnnic Service Station.

Photo by Monte Kelly

This modern office desk designed by Ann Maselli for **Nutshell News's** ''Room of the Month'' series is where the editor of **Nutshell News** writes and edits articles, reviews work submitted by craftspeople and slides of collections, and keeps in touch with hobbyists from coast to coast through two address-filled rolodexes.

Photo by Ann Maselli

I'd leave all the hurry,
the noise and the fray
For a house full of books
and a garden of flowers

—Andrew Long, I'd Leave

In this section of the prestigious Salk Institute, scientists study the brain's reaction to chemicals and the eventual effect on human behavior. Pat Kissel, a miniaturist and tour guide at the Institute, was fascinated by this particular stop on her weekly tour. With permission from the Institute staff, Pat and her husband Bill, a retired mechanical design engineer, duplicated the lab and its sophisticated scientific equipment in 1'' scale.

Photo courtesy of Dr. Floyd Bloom, Arthur Vining Davis Center for Behavioral Neurobiology

Architects may dream of towering buildings, but their plans start in small scale. In this Landscape Architect's Office built by the Robert Freeman family for the 1980 Philadelphia Flower Show, the architect is planning a garden for a tiny (144th scale) residence. The Freemans' ingenuity and technical skill make their entries favorites in the annual Flower Show. Bob Freeman, a math teacher and director of the IGMA Guild School, built most of the furnishings. His wife Dody painted the background scene and made many accessories. Daughter Lisa, a horticulturist, advised on the miniature plantings required for competition in the event.

The Bountiful Larder

"No matter where I serve my guests, they always like my kitchen best," the saying goes. Perhaps that's because the kitchen is a warm, inviting place where wonderful things happen. Some kitchens are of the chrome and tile variety, all stocked with the most modern gadgetry. In other kitchens, old biscuit tins line the counters, gleaming pots and pans decorate the walls, and herb-filled baskets hang from ceiling beams. No matter what its style, the kitchen is a spot where friends and family love to gather. From early morning coffee to midnight refrigerator raids, the kitchen brims with activity and can rightfully be called the heart of any home.

The kitchens featured here range from the 17th and 18th century Nuremberg versions used as instructional toys for little girls, to contemporary kitchens complete with food processors and microwave ovens.

The cooks who make the foods that fill these miniature kitchens are often creative full-size chefs as well. Before they try a new recipe in miniature, they test it in its full-size version. Miniature chef Barbara Meyer often does this, noting the measurements, colors, and textures of the real turkey or roast sitting on her kitchen table as she sculpts the 1" replica. Barbara says she struggled with miniature shrimp for months. Each time she was on the verge of capturing the crustacean's texture or coloring, her family members gobbled up her models!

While some miniature chefs work from full-size foods, others rely on color pictures in cookbooks for their inspirations. They study recipes because knowing the ingredients of a dish helps them understand what the finished food should look like. The ingredients for their miniature foods vary from bread dough to Sculpey, Fimo, wax, casting resins, glass beads, paper, even shredded sponge and crushed spices.

These cooks fold, grate, chop, blend, knead, boil, frost, whip, bake and garnish as enthusiastically as James Beard or Julia Child. They prepare full course meals, and some miniature cooks even give you authentic recipes for the tiny foods you purchase from them.

There are chefs who specialize in desserts, others who prefer canned goods or fresh fruits and vegetables, and some who rate five spoons for their regional dishes and holiday menus. Some miniaturists enjoy researching their meals, and they prepare feasts from specific periods in history. One such chef even supplies her customers with notes on the origins of her period foods.

The makers of these miniature delicacies are perfectionists who often go to the trouble of marbelizing meats or making individual cherries for pies, even though these details may not be seen in the finished product. The chef knows those finishing touches are there, and that is the proof of the pudding.

Miniature cooks also understand the importance of timing in the success of their recipes. Sylvia Clarke, who sells her small foods at shows, notes that she makes the most sales during the lunch hour when buyers are hungry. She recalls a show when a disgruntled and hungry husband was pulled to her table by his wife. "If you're hungry, take your choice," his wife told him. "You can have a BLT, hot dog, french fries. . ." "Where?!" he said, perking up. Then he realized his wife was referring to the miniature foods on the table in front of them.

One advantage to enjoying miniature foods is that they will never add inches to the waistline. You can marvel over the paper-thin translucence of a tiny head of lettuce, indulge in the rich, moist texture of a chocolate mocha torte, and almost smell the aroma of a hearty beef Wellington encased in its flaky pastry shell — and never need to count the calories. *Bon apetit!*

If all the world was apple-pie,
And all the sea was ink,
And all the trees were bread and cheese,
What should we have to drink?

The kitchen is often considered the center of a home, and that is certainly true here. It is the kids' first stop after school and — judging from the notes on the fridge — the message center for the household. NN's Special Projects Editor Bonnie Bennett built this contemporary kitchen modifying Scientific Miniatures' Realife kitchen cabinets and using Minis by M.E. appliances. Foods and other kitchen accessories came from numerous sources.

Photo by Shelby Harris

We may live without friends;
we may live without books;
But civilized man cannot live
without cooks

—Bulwer-Lytton

The Colonial tavern room offered warmth, hearty food, and strong ale to weary travelers. To showcase work by some of today's finest artisans, craftsperson and author Bettyanne Twigg created this historically accurate three-dimensional portrait of a wayside tavern in 1'' scale.

Collector and craftsperson Barbara Main based this kitchen on childhood memories of the kitchen in her family's home. The room was built with Jane Graber's crockery and Barbara's aged corner cupboard in mind. A mixture of painted Chrysnbon pieces and handcrafted items which Barbara customized finishes the scene.

Photo by Jill Riner

You find milk and I'll find flour,
And we'll have a pudding
In half an hour

Holidays are traditionally a time for feasting, and no seasonal meal was more temptingly prepared or elegantly served than the Christmas dinners of Charles Dickens' era. This meal, first shown on the cover of **Colonial Homes** magazine's December 1980 issue, was copied in 1'' scale by miniatures chef Barbara Meyer. Shown clockwise from left front are turnips, braised celery, crown roast ribs of beef, popovers, baked mashed potatoes, roast goose, cranberry relish, sherbets, herb pie, applesauce, oyster stew, boiled lobsters, and steamed green beans.

Photo by Chris Becker

A kitchen is only as good as its chef, and this cook sculpted in wax by Canadian dollmaker Arlyn Coad seems highly competent. Arlyn is a puppeteer who makes dolls when she and husband Luman are not performing. Using wax, Arlyn achieves the translucence of true flesh tones.

One of the coziest rooms in Jackie Barlow's Cape May Victorian dollhouse (pictured elsewhere in this book) is the kitchen decorated in Jackie's favorite red, white, and blue color scheme. The kitchen features a combination of antique and new pieces, including a copper stove and utensils made by Harry Littwin and foods prepared by Linda Warter.

Photo courtesy Jackie Barlow

What do you choose when you're offered a treat?
When Mother says, ``What would you like best to eat?''
—Christopher Morley, Animal Crackers

This inviting kitchen in the 16-room Grey Dollhouse, a ca. 1900 New England Colonial owned by Doris and Edgar Callahan, combines culinary accessories from several periods. The copper and brass stove and most of the copper utensils were made by the Callahans' son Robert.

Photo by Herb Randle

The State in Schulkyll is an exclusive, private men's club in Pennsylvania which dates to the 18th century. This room built by L. Rodman Page for the 1981 Philadelphia Miniature Show depicts the club's well-equipped kitchen.

Photo by Carol Tabas

I will make my kitchen, and you shall keep your room,
Where white flows the river and bright blows the broom

—Robert Louis Stevenson, I Will Make You Brooches

Contemporary settings like Jeanette Vines' kitchen create a rapport between viewer and scene because the viewer can relate to the room. Jeanette and her husband Dudley built "Dinner For Two" around Leslie Rahmatulla's copper, Francis Whittemore's glassware, and assorted kitchenware from Steak Family Miniatures. The scene suggests preparations for a special dinner.

Photo courtesy Jeanette and Dudley Vines

Jacquelyn and Jason Getzan are established miniatures artisans, primarily because of their copperware and cutlery. Both Getzans are full-size artists, and Jacquelyn's special talents have come to light in her 1″ pastries like this three-layer treat with glazed fruit toppping. Jason made the cake server.

The kitchen of Sebo Hall castle has been in use for 600 years. David Jones, who designed the room with help from owners Kate and Alex Sebo, combined the new and old in this kitchen. The original fireplaces have been filled with large ovens, a wood stove, radar oven, and barbecue. The island contains a dishwasher and working sink.

Photo courtesy Alex and Kate Sebo

The kitchen's the cosiest place that I know:
The kettle is singing, the stove is aglow

—Christopher Morley, Animal Crackers

Nuremberg, once the toy capitol of the world, gave its name to the small toy kitchens produced as educational toys for little girls during the 17th and 18th centuries. The kitchens were chockfull of the copper pots, pewter serving pieces, crockery and utensils needed by a housewife. This contemporary version of the Nuremberg kitchen was assembled by scientist, author, doll and miniatures collector Kathryn Clisby. Combining furnishing by contemporary artisan Warren Dick with antique pieces, Kathryn has modeled her kitchen on one in "Mon Plaisir," Duchess Augusta Dorothea's 18th century German dollhouse of some 84 rooms.

Photo by Jim Cook

The Irish never decline a meal of corned beef and cabbage, new potatoes, soda bread and green beer — all their native foods. This St. Patrick's Day pot 'o gold feast was prepared by Florida crafter Nancy Ranney for her "Picture Perfect Parties" do-it-yourself series in **Nutshell News.**

Collector and dealer Jackie Andrews of Andrews Miniatures used Chrysnbon Miniatures' furniture and accessory kits to complete this turn-of-the-century kitchen. This room is part of a seven-room house furnished throughout with Chrysnbon pieces.

❧ THE BOUNTIFUL LARDER ❧

When I have my house I will suit myself,
And have what I'll call my ``Condiment Shelf''
Filled with all manner of herbs and spice,
Curry and chutney for meats and rice

—Don Blanding, Vagabond House

Maggie Brown, an ex-journalist and teacher, and Sue Rice, a former antiques dealer and character doll maker, share a fondness for artist Carl Larsson's watercolors depicting interiors from his native Sweden. They recreated Larsson's version of an 1899 Scandinavian kitchen/dining area from the book **A Home** and captured third prize in the exhibit competition at the 1979 NAME National Houseparty in Boston.

The pie safe came by its name honestly, as a place to keep pies safe from insects, dust and between meal nibblers. Pierced metal door and side panels let air flow through the cabinet. This piece was built by Tom Martin who specializes in building functional miniatures.

Antique miniature foods were often molded from terra cotta, papier mache, wax, plaster, or glass. These wax foods and Majolica ware by Giustiniani are part of a collection of 17th and 18th century creche scenes owned by Jeffery Gueno and Frank Hanley. The Majolica platter with prosciutto has a pearl handled silver knife.

Photo courtesy Jeffery Gueno and Frank Hanley

Elegant Dining

In earlier times, the masses of civilization lived in what amounted to one "great room" where they cooked, ate, slept, and bathed (on occasion). What this arrangement lacked in privacy was made up for in cost and ease of construction, warmth, and overall practicality.

Life did not begin to take on a more comfortable aspect until early in the 18th century when divisions of labor and more organized production methods made the buying and selling of commodities not only possible but profitable.

As the middle class began to prosper, their dwellings became more private and complex in their layout, and rooms took on specific functions. The concept of a dining area as a separate room in the middle class home did not catch on until later in the 18th century. Until then, food was often served upstairs in the bed chamber.

As money flowed more freely in the 18th century, so did wine. Entertaining became fashionable, and the tools of this social art became more sophisticated. With the emergence of work by such renowned cabinetmakers as Sheraton, Hepplewhite, Adam and Duncan Phyfe, the dining room was graced by the addition of fine inlaid and veneered sideboards, knife boxes, wine coolers and tea caddies. Silversmiths in Philadelphia, Boston, and New York state hammered out classic pieces whose styles remain in demand today. Until Benjamin Bakewell founded his glass factory in Pittsburgh in 1808, the manufacture of clear cut and engraved glass had been unachievable in America. The beautiful glassware produced in this factory blended perfectly into the dining room's decor.

Blessed by the money to stock its butler's pantry and the craftsmanship to furnish its interior, the dining room became the heart of American hospitality. And it remained so until the advent of rec rooms and, more recently, the fully-equipped, computerized and digitized home entertainment center.

Regardless of style or period, the miniature dining room is often one of the more traditional rooms in the dollhouse. Its basic components include a table, chairs, sideboard, corner cupboard, ceiling light fixture, china, silver, glassware, and a flower arrangement or two. But take a closer look at some of the rooms featured in this chapter. They contain these standard elements, but they are by no means staid. By using vibrant colors, subtle textures, elegant furniture, and beautiful accessories, the decorators and craftspeople who have assembled these dining rooms have created a look that is uniquely their own. No doubt Emily Post would give each of them a silver spoon for style and elegance!

*I'm going to Lady Washington's,
To get a cup of tea
And five loaves of gingerbread,
So don't you follow me!*

—Nursery Rhyme, Eastern United States

This Federal style Charleston dining room was executed by Cincinnatian Jack Kuresman and is a tribute to his fine furniture building skills. Jack divides his free time between miniatures and occasional acting, and his flair for the "dramatic" comes across in this setting which showcases miniature silver by a number of well known artisans. Charles Tebelman, Jack's partner in miniatures work, made the silk needlepoint rug in the room.

Photo by Anne D. Smith

Robert Simms was a cabinetmaker and furniture restorer in England before coming to Virginia to work in a similar capacity for the Colonial Williamsburg Foundation. He and his son Richard began a miniatures business building classic pieces such as these mahogany knife boxes banded in ebony and holly. The 1" silverware is also theirs.

This Victorian dining room is part of a 12-room miniature home displayed at the White House during the 1981 Christmas season. For the project, interior designer Aline Gray assembled work by many artisans, including Helen Cohen who made over 40 dolls dressed in antique fabrics like these ladies. Aline's good taste in fine art, Oriental rugs and fabrics with the patina of age lends elegance to this setting.

Photo by Carol Tabas

❧ ELEGANT DINING ❧

Don't spill your tea, or gnaw your bread,
And don't tease one another;
And Tommy mustn't talk too much,
Or quarrel with his brother

—Kate Greenaway

Photo by Anne D. Smith

Jennifer and Herb Bennett are a Midwestern miniature-making couple who combine her ceramic and porcelain skills with his woodworking expertise. Jennifer designed these colorful dishes based on the Fiesta pattern first manufactured in 1936.

Marie Friedman is a highly versatile, knowledgeable craftsperson known particularly for her porcelain dinnerware. Each year, Marie designs one in an on-going series of miniature plates like this as gifts for special friends.

Photo by Marie Friedman

Mrs. James Ward Thorne's series of 1'' scale American and European rooms are considered by many to be the best existing examples of miniatures craftsmanship. This ca. 1940 New Mexico dining room was inspired by the missions and haciendas built in New Mexico in this century using American and European construction methods. The simple but substantial furniture is modeled on Mexican and Spanish prototypes. Much of the silver and pottery was found in Mexico City.

Photo courtesy the Art Institute of Chicago

*When I have a house . . . as I sometimes may . . .
I'll suit my fancy in every way*

—Don Blanding, Vagabond House

French chefs have long preferred copper cookware because of its even heating capability. In the dollhouse, gleaming copper pots and pans add rich color to a kitchen. These working pieces were made by Leslie Rahmatulla in 1'' and 1/2'' scales.

Tobacco was an economic mainstay of the 18th century South and brought wealth and power to the plantation owners who grew it. The plant was artistically rendered in an 18th century china pattern which New England potter Elizabeth Chambers has reduced to 1'' scale.

Book author, photographer, and gardener Ann Kimball Pipe builds most of her miniature rooms in 3/4'' to 1' scale, crafting most of her own furniture and accessories. She prefers rooms from the early 1900s, especially those with a lived in look. This oak dining room with carved buffet and claw-footed table is reminiscent of many seen during the early years of the 20th century.

Photo by Ann Kimball Pipe

God send us a little home,
To come back to, when we roam
—Florence Bone, A Prayer for a Little Home

Emily Good's career in science and mathematics is far afield from her miniatures work, but both require concentration and attention to detail. She is adept at construction, carving, turning, painting, needlework, and metal casting in 1" scale. Emily built everything in this vignette, including the 1810 silver tea and coffee service.

Photo by Emily Good

William H. and Frances Bowen are native Southerners, history buffs, and a husband/wife team who enjoy recreating historic American rooms in 1" scale. Most of their rooms like the Kinsley-Johns dining room from New Castle, DE, shown here, are built by William who devises his own tooling to make precise moldings, paneling, fireplaces, and some furniture. Frances uses her eye for quality workmanship to assemble the other furnishings for their rooms.

Photo courtesy William Harvey Bowen

Men once retired to the library after dinner to enjoy brandy and cigars while ladies took tea or light cordials in a separate salon. Joe Murter's ca. 1750-60 Queen Anne side chair with carved splat horseshoe back would grace either setting. Gerald Crawford's table is copied from a full-size piece in the Wintherthur Museum. The tea service is by Paul McNeely.

Tea trays, baskets ranged in order,
Plates, with alphabets 'round the border!
—William Brighty Rands, The Peddler's Caravan

Thanks to rich deposits of silver and gold, the West has always attracted artisans working in precious metals. Arizona artists Tom Gilbert and Lexi Samuels bring skill in jewelry making, sculpture, and metalsmithing to their miniature designs like this one-of-a-kind gold tea service.

Richard Prillaman is a full-size silversmith and instructor who became intrigued with miniatures through one of his students who was also a hobbyist. Some of Richard's 1" scale silver is shown here.

Photo by Ellen Krucker Blauer

The dining room in John and Ellen Blauer's 42-room Maynard Manor is a marriage of Victorian Revival, Louis XVI, and Flemish decor. The fabric wallpaper resembles that used by Marie Antoinette in her bedroom and was part of a limited run made by Burlington Mills in the 1960s. The dining table holds numerous silver serving pieces from the Florence Bentley collection. The Victorian curio cabinets flanking the china cabinet are from the Mother Larke collection and hold rare Limoges pieces.

Pewter and bronze and hammered brass,
Old carved wood and gleaming glass,
All of the beautiful, useless things
That a vagabond's aimless drifting brings

—Don Blanding, Vagabond House

New Mexico jeweler Pete Acquisto began making 1'' silver miniatures in 1980 after being introduced to the dollhouse hobby by his sister Jeannette Vines, a collector and crafter. Pete uses the lost wax casting method to make items like this chalice and baby cup. His pieces are authentic replicas of full-size originals, many from the 18th century.

Master artisan Francis Whittemore has been involved in glass blowing for over 40 years, working in miniature scale for much of that time. Years spent in scientific glass blowing eventually led to his making art glass paperweights which have been displayed and sold through major museums in the US. These etched glass pieces represent a few of the many new designs Francis introduces each year.

Full-size silversmith and woodcarver Jean Boardman prefers to forge rather than cast her mostly one-of-a-kind silver miniatures. This silver tea service took Jean 150 hours to complete. The teapot has a flanged, removable lid and its spout pours.

The beams of my house will be fragrant wood
That once in a teeming jungle stood

—Don Blanding, Vagabond House

This china featured on NN's December 1983 cover was made by Jean Yingling, a miniaturist for almost 10 years who is known for the translucence and fine detailing of her work.

Your dining room is much more than a table, chairs and a hutch. The clever use of color and accessories can give your dining area a unique character. Dee Snyder used bottle green with Colonial red accents as her color scheme in this country setting. Stenciled wallpaper, folk toys, a rag rug, ''ironstone'' crockery, and a punched tin chandelier complete the scene.

Photo by Dee Snyder

John and Ellen Blauer have collected miniatures for over 30 years, and their Maynard Manor collection includes many fine pieces purchased abroad, from private collections, or from contemporary craftspeople. Shown here is an 18-piece gold coffee service in the Manor's dining room.

Photo by Ellen Blauer

Let others delight 'mid new pleasure to roam,
But give me, oh, give me, the pleasures of home

—John Hayward Paine, Home, Sweet Home

Miniature silversmith Obadiah Fisher made these 1''
versions of an 18th century silver teapot with brazier
and a Monteith bowl used for chilling drinking glasses.

Sgraffito ware is decorative earthenware characterized
by pictures and sayings scratched through a surface
glaze to reveal the earthenware beneath. The first sgraffito ware in America came from England in the 17th
century. These 1'' sgraffito pieces were made by Lee-
Ann Chellis-Wessell.

Photo by Sarah Salisbury

Over the years, the 1'' porcelain dinnerware, accessories and foods made by
potter Debbie McKnight have set a standard for fine craftsmanship. These
Canton pieces were made by Debbie and painted by Priscilla Lance. The
lion's head, claw-footed pedestal table was made by New Mexico artisan
Lynn Jons-Kaysing.

Judy Beckwith's success as a miniature painter intrigued her husband
Jim who increased his participation in Judy's business from picture framer
to metalsmith. Since 1979, Jim has developed his own line of fine turned
brass accessories like these candlesticks, ginger jars, bowls and plates.

There's a cake full of plums, there are strawberries too,
And the table is set on the green

—Kate Greenaway

The archives of Philadelphia's Drexel University Museum contain the extensive miniatures collection of alumna Marjorie Ellis Kroha. These ca. 1927 silver miniature serving pieces are part of her vast collection of accessories.

Photo by Peter Groesbeck

This casual dining scene called "Strawberries on the Patio" uses the bright red summer fruit as its decorating theme. Folk artist Susan Forrest painted tiny strawberries on the deacon's bench, chest, and serving pieces, and wove berries through the chandelier. The break-away box captured the Best Craftsmanship award in the Columbia, MO Miniature Guild's Break-Away Box Contest.

Photo by Barbara Warner

Gudrun Kolenda hand throws lovely ceramic ware from elegant 30-piece dinner sets to utilitarian shaving mugs. These flower-decorated dishes are part of a Victorian set.

A Room Of One's Own

Britite author Virginia Woolf understood the importance of having a room of one's own and even wrote a novel on the subject. Having a special retreat that is yours alone — a private place where you can be at peace — is vitally important in a stress-filled world that constantly jangles the nerves. The most important aspect of this private space is that it be filled with things that bring you joy. Good books, thick carpeting, a fireplace and comfortable chair, music, small treasures collected over the years, family photographs, fresh flowers, a typewriter and colorful pens and stationery would comprise my private hideaway.

But your special place need not be elaborate, nor does it require four walls. I know someone whose retreat is the back porch of her home where she sips her coffee every morning, listening to the birds and watching the world wake up. A Chopin concerto can transport yet another friend to a private and serene world. A child's favorite place might be under a tree where he or she can pretend that the low hanging branches are the walls of a tepee or the sails of a pirate ship.

Quiet moments spent thinking or daydreaming in a room of one's own are not wasted, because they refresh the creative spirit and restore the mental and physical energy needed to tackle the world — and all those unfinished hobby projects!

It comes as no surprise that miniaturists rank assembling and decorating miniature rooms second only to building dollhouses as their do-it-yourself preference. If your home is already bursting at the seams and the only private space you might conceivably retreat to is the bathroom or the linen closet, create a miniature getaway and enjoy it vicariously each time you look at it on the mantel, bookshelf or coffee table.

Miniature rooms are easier and less time consuming to construct than dollhouses, so the beginning hobbyist doesn't become discouraged, and the pro doesn't become bored. Rooms take up less space, require less financial investment, are lighter in weight, and lend themselves to interesting displays.

Miniaturists approach room building and decorating in a variety of ways. Some hobbyists prefer to research and build historic interiors. Others gravitate to rooms from literature or photos in magazines. Still others close their eyes and let imagination take them where it will. Rooms depicting a workplace, hobby workshop or other significant setting are often given as gifts. Rooms are frequently made to duplicate full-size interiors which hold sentimental value. And many rooms are created out of pure wish fulfillment; these are truly the private rooms of one's own.

Despite their boxy structure, miniature rooms don't box in your creativity or ingenuity. The same kit room can be modified or bashed in countless ways to become a shop, fairy grotto, royal boudoir, or a city penthouse. All it takes is a little time spent daydreaming, and before you know it you will be inspired to create anything from a strictly authentic period room to a magical sorcerer's den.

He is happiest, be he king or peasant
who finds peace in his home

—Goethe

New Jersey artisans Norma Slominski and Chuck Krug designed this tastefully decorated contemporary room with concessions to classic French styling. The room captured second prize in the 1983 Philadelphia Flower Show miniature room competition. The exhibit theme was ''Noonday Sun,'' with categories divided into spring/summer and fall/winter scenes. Norma, a miniature furniture builder, and Chuck, a painter, chose warm shades of green and pumpkin to play out the fall theme.

Photo by Ron McNally

❧ A ROOM OF ONE'S OWN ❧

Our little house is a friendly house,
It is not shy or vain
—Christopher Morley, Song for a Little House

The 1″ scale plantation office from Carter's Grove near Williamsburg, VA, closely duplicates the full-size restoration. The 19-room miniature mansion was built by Dr. Charles Holcomb for Elizabeth Carter Marvin, a descendant of King Carter, builder of the original plantation. The Colonial Williamsburg Foundation cooperated by opening the house to the miniaturists for after hours tours, photo sessions, and close inspections of furnishings. The miniature Carter's Grove is now part of the Jackie and Joe Andrews collection.

Photo by David Herrema

Miniature rooms are not restricted to certain historic periods, and more and more miniaturists are building settings which reflect the way we live today. Professional architectural scale modeler Peter Westcott built this spacious contemporary living room to show the possibilities available in modern style furnishings.

Photo courtesy Peter Westcott

Because of their never-ending love affair with Mexico, George and Jeanne Munoz specialize in miniature furniture and accessories with a Mexican flair. This courtyard with terra cotta tile floor and working fountain is similar to the one in the Munozes' own home. The equipales — leather and wood chairs seen throughout Mexico — and the accessories are all authentic reproductions of full-size pieces found during the couple's frequent trips to Mexico.

🐦 A ROOM OF ONE'S OWN 🐦

For I'll have good friends who can sit and chat
Or simply sit, when it comes to that,
By the fireplace where the fir logs blaze
And the smoke rolls up in a weaving haze

—Don Blanding, Vagabond House

Miniatures have been a way of life for collectors Jack and Shirley Bloomfield since 1975, and the couple is known for their good taste and enthusiasm for the hobby. This room built for the Bloomfields by Lorraine Scuderi-Lamagra is what the pair say they would want in a second, getaway home: a traditional room filled with stylish and comfortable pieces.

Author and miniatures expert Flora Gill Jacobs founded the Washington Dolls' House and Toy Museum in 1975 as a showcase of antique miniature dollhouses, dolls, toys and games. Here, Madame St. Quentin stands in the parlor of her 15-room English dollhouse built between 1856-58 on an estate near Burford, England by the estate's carpenter. Most furnishings here are later than the house itself and include cast iron and Biedermeier pieces.

Photo courtesy the Washington Dolls' House & Toy Museum

69

Oh, keep a place apart
Within your heart,
For little dreams to go

—Louise Driscoll, Hold Fast Your Dreams

Photo by John Wyatt

English watercolorist Patience Arnold has given over part of her home to a museum of over 20 antique and contemporary dollhouses. Although her interest in dollhouses began in her childhood, Patience's adult collecting began in 1969 with the purchase of the 1885 Heversham House, above, complete with most of its original furniture and dolls.

Photo by Ellen Krucker Blauer

The French Room in Maynard Manor is a tribute to the extravagances of the reign of King Louis XVI and Marie Antoinette. This is a lady's room and mirrors the influence the young queen had on French tastes of the period. Ellen Blauer made almost all the furniture in the room using brass with a 24K gold-plated finish. Limoges and cloisonne accessories, ivory and Battersea furniture, silk and satin upholstery fabric, painted wallpaper, and gilt mirrors, moldings and trim complete the elegant setting.

You are going out to tea to-day,
So mind how you behave;
Let all accounts I have of you
Be pleasant ones, I crave

—Kate Greenaway

Photo by Raymond Knapp

The inhabitants of the parlor in this ca. 1860 English dollhouse are about to enjoy tea served from a rare service of vaseline-colored Bohmer dishes. The six-room house furnished with ormulu pieces, Dore bronzes, ivory and Biedermeier furniture and over 30 dollhouse dolls is owned by long-time collectors Hazel and Raymond Knapp.

Photo courtesy the Miniature Museum of Kansas City

Thanks to the diverse tastes of collectors Mary Harris Francis and Barbara Marshall, the Miniature Museum of Kansas City, opened in 1982, boasts a well-rounded display of both antique and contemporary miniatures. This parlor from the Josephine Bird Hall dollhouse contains all its original, turn-of-the-century furniture including many paintings on ivory and ormulu-style pieces from the German toy manufacturer Marklin.

Fools build houses, and wise men buy them

—English Proverb

Despite its practical nature, the form of a bath need not be slave to its function, as this luxurious retreat shows. This bath features a draped, marbelized sunken tub, stained glass windows, chandelier, caviar and wine — for two. Susan Sirkis designed the room specially for **Nutshell News** and executed it with contributions from numerous contemporary artisans.

Photo by Shelby Harris

I'm glad our house is a little house,
Not too tall nor too wide

—Christopher Morley, Song for a Little House

Artisan team Donald Dube and Linda Wexler-Dube created this ''Night Before Christmas'' contemporary living room and a companion dining room in 1980 for Christmas display in Cartier's Fifth Avenue store windows. The elegant room combines touches of French, Oriental, and contemporary style and was designed to show miniatures as an art form. Influenced by the Thorne Rooms, the pair built their rooms at an angle with half-hidden hallways and exterior scenes, and framed the viewing area with columned archways which lend a more intimate and theatrical dimension. Linda says the room is a culmination of all her back issues of **Architectural Digest**.

Photo courtesy Wexler-Dube Miniatures

It ain't home t' ye, though it be the palace of a king,
Until somehow yer soul is sort o' wrapped round everything

—Edgar A. Guest, Home

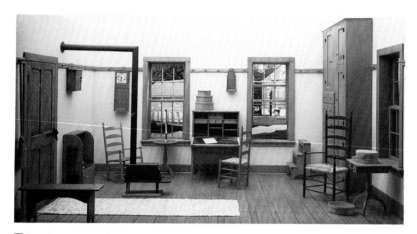

The religious sect known as the Shakers lent its name to the primitive furniture seen here. The utilitarian design of pieces built by Shaker craftspeople, and the simplicity of decoration in their interiors distinguish this style. Miniaturist James Ison specializes in primitive American furniture and settings like this ca. 1840 Shaker Elders Room.

Photo courtesy James Ison

Jim Marcus's towering Russian Embassy is a benchmark of fine miniature craftsmanship. In the parlor of this dollhouse, shown above, Jim strikes an impressive balance between massive furniture, plush fabrics, commanding woodwork and ornate ceiling and flooring designs.

Photo by Jim Marcus

Creator Betty Gleeson describes this 1'' setting as ''an American contemporary room with Oriental overtones.'' The scene evolved from a visit to Queen Mary's Dolls' House and Betty's longstanding love for Oriental furnishings. The physical layout was determined by her desire for floating stairs leading to a conversational sofa grouping. Betty built or kit bashed all the room's furniture, often using reworked rummage sale and dime store finds as accessories. Silver, ivory and jade curios are placed throughout the room, reminiscent of Betty's travels. Subtle colors, soft lighting, and curving lines enhance the tranquil Eastern atmosphere.

Photo by Yvonne Pessel

❧ A ROOM OF ONE'S OWN ❧

And I am praying to God on high,
And I am praying Him night and day,
For a little house — a house of my own —
Out of the wind's and the rain's way

—Padraic Colum, Old Woman of the Roads

This proper Victorian widow lives quietly in a bed-sitting room in the home of her son and his family. The room with its mass of Victorian clutter was designed by Judee Williamson to accommodate Michigan artisan Judy Shellhaas's intricately carved furniture. Judee Williamson executed all fabric treatments, and Judy Shellhaas built the furniture.

Photo by Shelby Harris

For 'tis always fair weather
When good fellows get together

—Richard Hovey, Spring

A *man's home is his castle, even when it's called "The Swamp" and is shared by three glib Army doctors from the former television series M*A*S*H.* **Vietnam veteran Bob Mosier built the set in miniature using an Army laundry bag as the cover for the 15" high tent. To research the layout, Bob used a 20th Century Fox book with photos of the set,** *and then watched the show religiously, determining all the room's measurements based on the actors' approximate heights.*

Photo by Charles Claudon

Eugene J. Kupjack has been a miniaturist for over 45 years. His contributions to the Thorne Rooms and the creation of over 700 rooms of his own have been well documented. Mr. Kupjack works with his sons Hank and Jay on projects ranging from rooms and vignettes to silver collectables. Many Kupjack projects are replicas of full-size, historically significant rooms, such as the blue and gold Flag Room at the Betsy Ross Memorial home in Philadelphia. The room reflects a strict sense of symmetry and balance — elements stressed by the late Mrs. James Ward Thorne, designer of the Thorne Rooms.

Photo by Jay Kupjack

❧ A ROOM OF ONE'S OWN ❧

I *remember, I remember,*
The house where I was born,
The little window, where the sun
Came peeping in at morn

—Thomas Hood, I Remember, I Remember

New Jersey artisan Nic Nichols is irresistibly drawn to the Victorian era with its swirling lines, ornate carving, and rich upholstery and draperies. His first room, this ca. 1850-1870 Beacon Hill parlor, captured first place at the 1979 NAME National Houseparty in Boston, MA. Nic completed the box, furniture, rug and draperies. A former department store display director, Nic brings an element of drama to the settings he designs with the help of his wife Linda. The portrait above the sofa is Nic himself.

Jeanne Knoop believes that miniatures let you bring far away places to life. Although she has never been to Tahiti, Jeanne has created a tropical paradise in her miniature Tahitian room. An antiques collector, miniature crafter and a graduate of the New York School of Interior Design, Jeanne has built over 80 rooms. She combines antiques with contemporary pieces, and handcrafted items with commercial ones — all to achieve the desired effect.

Classic Designs

Who would dare to improve on such works of art as Charles Le Brun's baroque interiors at Versailles, Chippendale's ball and claw carving, Tiffany's favrile glass, or da Vinci's Mona Lisa? A thing of beauty is indeed a joy forever, as these masterpieces demonstrate. The artisan's creative vision as seen through these classic designs continues to thrill, awe, and inspire us centuries later. This is the essence of good design: that its beauty and appeal live on, regardless of trends or fads.

The individual pieces and collective rooms featured in this chapter represent some of the finest, most creative and innovative designs the miniatures world has to offer. Some are rare antiques, others are contemporary pieces. Many of the objects shown here represent specific interests within the hobby. The prominence of such classic styles as Victorian, Queen Anne, William and Mary, Chippendale, and Shaker is not a matter of coincidence. Surveyed readers of **Nutshell News** prefer these styles above all others, with Victorian ranking number one and traditional 18th century designs running a close second.

You will recognize many of the artisans whose work is featured here because they have gained a reputation over the years for expert craftsmanship. Some have been making miniatures for a decade or longer and helped establish the standards of quality which have elevated the hobby to an art form. The names of other craftspeople will be less familiar, but their work is equally inspired.

Many of the miniatures chosen for this chapter deserve recognition not only because of the craftsmanship they exhibit, but because they are innovative, unique, and creative approaches to working in 1'' scale. With the legacy of so many talented artisans to draw on, no doubt the world of miniatures in both its hobby and art forms will achieve even greater levels of creativity.

Spend all you have for loveliness,
Buy it and never count the cost

—Sara Teasdale, Barter

Pieces of this delicately carved ivory furniture are often seen in older dollhouses. John and Ellen Blauer, owners of this dressing table and stool, traced the furniture's origins to a Swiss firm which produced the pieces from about 1900 to 1930.

Photo by Ellen Krucker Blauer

Marilyn Monroe — a legend on and off the screen — is captured here by doll artist Delores Coles in a classic pose from the movie "The Seven Year Itch." Working in combinations of Sculpey and Fimo, Delores makes a wide variety of poseable character dolls including toddlers and ethnic figures.

Don Buttfield has contributed greatly to the miniatures hobby as an artisan and an active member and former president of IGMA. His six-legged stand for a Chinese fish bowl made by Debbie McKnight and Priscilla Lance was part of the 1979 IGMA auction.

Life has loveliness to sell,
All beautiful and splendid things

—Sara Teasdale, Barter

Antique playthings offer rich glimpses into yesteryear, reflecting the lifestyles of the adults who built them and the children who enjoyed them. New Yorker Ann Anthony built this Pavillion in 1769 at the age of 14. She dressed the German dolls and modeled the wax animals in the setting. (Gift of Ruth A. Child)

Photo courtesy the Museum of the City of New York

Margaret Woodbury Strong began collecting miniatures in the early 1900s, and collections of all types became a lifelong passion. When she died in 1969, Mrs. Strong owned a staggering number of objects, including 27,000 dolls and over 600 dollhouses. The core of these collections is assembled in a portrayal of American daily life from 1830-1930 in the Rochester, NY, museum which bears Mrs. Strong's name. Shown here is a German dollhouse with original wallpaper and simulated tile floors. This six-room house with bay windows and elevator is one of the most outstanding antique houses in the collection.

Photo courtesy the Margaret Woodbury Strong Museum

In the early 1970s, Jim Holmes was a pioneer in the building of authentic American primitive furniture — the older and more distressed the better. This dry sink and child's chair are more recent pieces which depict Jim's talent for developing aged finishes.

Ernie Levy makes authentic reproductions of unusual full-size furniture. His French pre-Victorian dressing table in walnut and cherry features a beveled glass mirror supported by swan arms, an Italian marble top, and lyre motif leg supports.

All these things I will have about,
Not a one could I do without
—Don Blanding, Vagabond House

Whether they deliver someone to the church on time or await passengers outside a fashionable mansion, Conrad Smith's conveyances are elegance personified. Working from measurements he takes of full-size vehicles in carriage museums, Conrad builds his 1″ versions from maple, brass and leather, recreating the vehicle right down to the carriage bolts.

Photo courtesy Conrad Smith

Miniature furniture builder Linda LaRoche prefers to use dense grained fruitwoods and hand tools for her Chippendale and Hepplewhite pieces. She also makes her own hardware. Shown here is Linda's carved rosewood Victorian chair.

Photo courtesy Linda LaRoche

Physical therapist David White loves aged American country furniture. He and his wife Jody restore such pieces for their home, so it was natural that David build country furniture when he tried miniature making. Using multiple washes of color and light rubbing techniques, David creates the distressed look of pieces like this bun-footed chest.

Clifford Yerks builds primitive furniture of Shaker origin. Although confined to a wheelchair, Cliff pursues an active miniatures business, and his work is represented in several museums. Using maple, cherry and pine, Cliff refers to photos from books and magazines to make over 25 Shaker furniture items.

But strange stored-away things
Not like everyday things
Make marvelous playthings
From attics and such

—Dorothy Brown Thompson, I Like Housecleaning

George and Joan Passwaters became miniaturists through an interest in antique toys. George noticed the trend toward miniatures in 1965 and started making Queen Anne and William and Mary pieces, primarily. A professional model maker who has simulated everything from rockets to underwater housings for cameras, George finds 1″ scale relaxing after working daily with objects one-tenth of a thousandth of an inch small. Shown here are two of his chairs.

Puerto Rican born Ibes Gonzales has played in a Latin jazz band, driven a taxi, and studied every craft from pottery to woodworking. His first love is carving in miniature which he began in 1978. Using chisels ground specially for miniatures work, Ibes carves pieces like this Chippendale chair with satinwood veneer and eagle motif across its top rail. He carved a shell and vine design on the center section of the Chippendale low boy.

Photo by Anne D. Smith

Hermanian Anslinger is a talented artisan who keeps a low profile. Working from full-size measurements, she built this Wooten secretary with black walnut exterior and burled veneer insets. (Blauer Collection)

Photo by Ellen Krucker Blauer

❧ CLASSIC DESIGNS ❧

I know a little cupboard,
With a teeny tiny key
And there's a jar of Lollipops
For me, me, me

—Walter de la Mare, The Cupboard

The clean lines and rich heritage of Shaker furniture appeal to many miniaturists, including Jim Hastrich and Renee Bowen who have studied full-size pieces extensively at Sabbathday Lake, ME, one of two surviving communities founded by this religious sect. Their ca. 1890 Elder Henry Green sewing desk is considered a classic Shaker piece and it is one of the couple's favorites, both in miniature and full-size.

Photo by Anne D. Smith

Mel Prescott, maker of this classic roll-arm fainting couch, was a miniaturist long before the hobby's current popularity. She introduced the glass-topped curio table and her version of the Queen Anne wingback chair two decades ago. Also shown are colored etchings by Jane Coneen, 22-mesh canvas pillows by Liz Adams, and dolls by Carol Spence.

Across the border in Canada, miniaturists have regional furniture styles which reflect their colonial heritage — the light woods and sturdy lines of Canadiana. John Ottewill specializes in old Ontario pieces like this ca. 1840-60 pine corner cupboard.

Photo by Anne D. Smith

To *have a clock with weights and chains*
And pendulum swinging up and down!

—Padraic Colum, Old Woman of the Roads

When tackling a new miniatures project, furniture builder Norma Slominski divides the piece into segments, working on one area at a time. Shown here are her Empire style, painted lyre back settee and chairs.

Photo by Ron McNally

Robert Chucka began making miniatures in 1977 at age 15. Bob credits his woodcarving grandfather with his talents for building 1" scale furniture, particulary Chippendale pieces like this side chair from the Governor's Palace in Colonial Williamsburg, VA. Note the delicately carved knees and feet on the piece.

Bill Robertson began making miniatures in 1975 when he was 19 and is one of a growing group of young craftspeople who are pursuing full-time careers in miniature making. Limited edition pieces like his working Elnathan Tabor clock have earned him the reputation of being an exacting and highly talented artisan.

*She hadn't a thing to sit on
But sofas and chairs I'm told,
And no other bed but a big one
That shone like an altar with gold!*

—Rafael Pombo, Columbian Nursery Rhyme

A *former elementary school teacher, Ivan Lawson became a miniaturist when illness forced an early retirement. Starting with balsa, Ivan progressed to hardwoods but still prefers to carve his pieces rather than use power tools. He is adept at woodworking, caning, rushing, and upholstery and often copies family heirlooms in miniature.*

Harry Smith is a painter, illustrator, book author, and woodworker who has worked in small scales for over 25 years. His miniatures have been exhibited at New York's prestigious Coe-Kerr art gallery and are considered fine art collectables. Shown here is his Cuban mahogany chest on chest.

Photo by Schecter Me Sun Lee

Even as a child during the 1950s, John Masterman built miniatures from balsa scraps. It was not until he saw the Thorne Rooms in 1971 that he realized the sophistication of the art and applied his full talents to pieces like this Chinese Chippendale curio cabinet built from satinwood.

*I'll have on a table a rich brocade
That I think the pixies must have made*

—Don Blanding, Vagabond House

Another example of 1'' scale Louis XV styling is British artisan Denis Hillman's tableaecrie and jewel coffer. Made from tulip and purple-wood, the coffer contains intricate inlays and porcelain-based enamel plaques. The oak and purplewood veneered tableaecrie has a tulip and purplewood parquet top and sides made from 3000 separate pieces of wood.

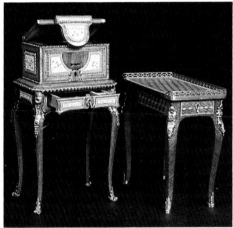

Design engineer Douglas Kirtland loves to whittle and takes his jack-knife and set of small files with him on lunch and coffee breaks to help him relax. The products of these whittling breaks are eventually assembled into 1'' scale, authentic reproductions of pieces like this Old Barracks flax spinning wheel.

California artisan Jim Marcus may be singlehandedly responsible for starting the rage in the 1970s for ornate Victorian miniature homes. His three-story Russian Embassy with its impressive tower was among the first 1'' scale renditions of San Francisco's "painted ladies."

> *My house is red — a little house,*
> *A happy child am I,*
> *I laugh and play the livelong day*
> *I hardly ever cry*

—Kate Greenaway

Former muscian, Naval officer, environmentalist, and copywriter Don Buckley left an ad agency career behind in the early 1970s to make his hobby of collecting American country antiques into a full-time business. Don and his wife Gloria sell full-size antique furniture and make similar pieces in 1″, 2″ and 3″ scales for miniaturists. This is Don's all-time favorite room, The Sunshine Inn Tavern, which he developed from a book on Connecticut's country inns. The room is the perfect setting for Don's high-style ca. 1690-1730 country furniture.

Although she was brought up in Santa Fe, doll artist Marty Saunders now lives in New England — home of many of the staunch, distinctly American types she sculpts in porcelain. A former portrait painter and theatrical costume designer, Marty takes her figures with their cloth-covered, wire armature bodies from real life. The pair here were inspired by paintings by John Singleton Copley.

This 12-room Octagon House is a total departure from Noel and Pat Thomas's Northwest Carpenter Gothic dollhouses. The house with its shingled dome went against every structural procedure the talented Washington State builders had ever used. The couple worked on the house from the center out, loosely basing their design on a ca. 1860 house in upstate New York. The miniature features fan-shaped rooms and a full basement.

❧ CLASSIC DESIGNS ❦

*And it's come away
to the land of fay,
That the katydid is singing*

—Eugene Field, Fairy and Child

A transplanted New Englander now living in California, school teacher Barbara Davis has collected full-size antique country furniture for years. In 1977, she began making similar pieces in miniature. To create the well-worn patina she loves, Barbara gave this bun-footed apothecary's chest numerous hand rubbings.

Before Kent Halstead became a career miniaturist, he apprenticed himself to an architectural restorations firm. While he reworked full-size homes during the day, he built a 1'' Victorian dollhouse at night. After five years, he went on his own as a miniaturist. One of his passions is building 1'' scale clocks. This working pillar and scroll clock with broken pediment is a favorite.

Photo by Marie Friedman

Stan Lewis made his debut in miniatures in 1980 when he was in his early twenties, but he had built small things for years. During a tour of historic Southern homes, Stan fell in love with Belter pieces and later tried them in miniature. He now builds the furniture in 1'' scale using Belter's veneer techniques and rare authentic patterns.

*It don't make any differunce how rich ye get t' be,
How much yer chairs an' tables cost, how great yer luxury*

—Edgar A. Guest, Home

Janna Joseph designs 1" scale dolls in complete, kit, and mold form, and has gained distinction through her likenesses of antique dolls and personalities from stage and literature. Her Jazz Age doll, below, wears a replica of a dress by designer Erte.

Artisan Harry Cooke calls his miniature work a "retirement hobby," but his elaborately constructed furniture like this bombe front secretary belie his modesty. Harry's pieces are done on a strictly limited commission-only basis, and are recognized as some of the finest contemporary works of art in the miniatures field.

Photo by Sherman Howe

The French influence is being seen more and more in miniature. Terry Rogal's carved Louis XV chair with caned insets is proof that the graceful lines of the French style translate successfully into 1" scale.

Photo by Terry Rogal

Smaller Measures, Greater Pleasures

Small, smaller, smallest — the uninitiated are often hard-pressed to tell the difference, but to the trained eye of a miniaturist, differences in size among small objects are so obvious that they are divided into distinct scales.

Miniatures have been made in varying sizes for centuries, but it is only recently that specific scales have been standardized. The most popular scale for dollhouse miniatures is 1″ equals 1′, but sizes abound on both ends of the spectrum.

Salesmen's samples and doll furniture are typical of larger scale furnishings from previous centuries. These furnishings in 2″, 3″ and larger scales are often displayed as case pieces and are cherished for their craftsmanship.

The demand on the craftsperson to achieve greater detail is what draws some artisans to scales larger than 1″. A tiny flaw which may go unnoticed in 1″ scale is magnified as size increases.

The scales of primary interest to miniaturists, however, fall on the smaller end of the measuring stick: 1/2″, 3/4″, 1/4″, 1/8″, even 1/16″ equals 1′.

In the 16th and 17th centuries, small scale English Battersea furniture, French Limoge pieces, and Dutch silver miniatures were abundant. In this century, America's Strombecker furniture, Sweden's Lundby line, plastic Renwal pieces, Petite Princess Fantasy Furniture, and the Princess Patti line were manufactered in 3/4″ scale.

Because interest in the miniatures world seems to be moving once again toward diminishing scales, the July 1982 issue of **Nutshell News** was devoted to the "Small Scale Revolution." For this issue, our staff canvased the commercial and collector markets in an effort to understand the fascination with smaller scales and to see what products were available.

We found that the general fascination with small objects increases as their size decreases. "Small things are cute, but smaller things are even cuter," one miniaturist observed. The size of these smaller objects seems to add to their charm and give them a certain magical quality. Smaller scales lend themselves to whimsical treatments which offer a welcome change of pace from more formal period room settings.

Change of pace and the challenge to make realistic-looking pieces in smaller scale are important factors in understanding the fascination with sizes smaller than 1″ equals 1′. We found that miniaturists most likely to be intrigued by smaller scales are those who have been active in the hobby for some time and who have already completed one 1″ dollhouse. Some of these people are long-time miniaturists who began their collections 10 to 15 years ago when few commercial dollhouse products were available. They became do-it-yourselfers then and now welcome the chance to put their contriving skills back into practice. Some are craftspeople who view smaller scale construction as a challenge and a chance to switch focus from functional realism to illusion. A builder working in 1″ scale can make drawers open, doors swing, pianos play, clocks keep time, and teapots pour: Form and function can go hand in hand. Smaller scales call for different adaptations which require the craftsperson to concentrate on what a piece looks like, not how it works.

Smaller scale objects also lend themselves to creative display treatments such as a country kitchen inside a teapot or a moonshine still inside a little brown jug. Because these displays are smaller and usually lightweight, they can be hung on a wall, placed on a narrow shelf, or displayed on a fireplace mantel. They take up less space than a 1″ dollhouse — an important consideration in this age of townhouse and condominium living. Some hobbyists even find smaller scale pieces easier to build since they require thinner woods and fewer power tools, and can even be made from paper or heavy cardboard.

The number of products available in smaller scales increases yearly, and many model railroading items in sizes comparable to 1/4″ and 1/8″ scale can be successfully adapted to dollhouse use. The greatest need is for more small scale accessories, bathroom fixtures, and modern kitchen appliances. While 1/2″ and smaller scales may never replace 1″ scale as the norm, these charming, diminutive miniatures are, as one hobbyist commented, "definitely here to stay."

And you shall have a tiny house,
A beehive full of bees,
A little cow, a largish cat,
And green sage cheese

—Kate Greenaway

Photo by David Gooley

Houses like Jay and Jackie McMahan's 1/2'' scale Rancho El Contento take up less space in a collection than a 1'' dwelling, but still allow the owner numerous decorating options. When 1/2'' furnishings are chosen with a careful eye for smaller proportions, the sense of realism can remain intact. The McMahans received this house built by Australian-born Sonny King as a surprise gift from their four daughters. The house is modeled on the McMahan's full-size home shown in the background. The house took Mr. King, a television director-designer for special effects, 31 months to build, and it is a striking replica of the original, right down to paint colors, brick patterns, and custom cabinetry. The McMahans celebrated the house's completion in 1981 with a gala ``open house'' on the lawn of their Brentwood, CA home.

When we prepared our July 1982 smaller scales issue, it was fairly easy to assemble standard room groupings, but what about settings beyond the usual living, dining and bedroom arrangements? To our pleasant surprise, we found 1/2'' rec room pieces, lawn furniture, wicker, gazebos and plants — even the pool and patio items shown here, made by Precision West Technology, Lovely Little Homes, Whitehead and Associates, and others.

❧ SMALLER MEASURES, GREATER PLEASURES ❧

Oh, that little toy land, I like it much,
That prim little, trim little, land of the Dutch!

—Olive Beaupre Miller, The Little Toy Land of the Dutch

Many miniaturists find tiny houses irresistible, as **Nutshell News** Associate Editor Dee Snyder reported in her February 1983 Collectables column. These small dwellings can be classed as toys, ornaments, souvenirs, or as functional objects like incense burners, banks, or decorative gift boxes. While there is no special scale for these structures, those in the "collectable" category usually fit in the palm of one's hand.

Former police officer-turned-lawyer Larry Steorts spends about two weeks building his delicately constructed houses using only an X-Acto knife, basswood scraps and toothpicks he turns by hand. Professing a secret desire to be an architect, Larry incorporates such structural details as interior stairways, window sashes, railings and wraparound porches into these four-inch wide houses which contain an average of 500 individual pieces.

Southern California miniaturists Norm and Jane Parker are experts in smaller scale building: to date, they have completed over 40 1/4" scale mansions like this 14-room Queen Anne style Victorian with semicircular wrap-around porch, turret with witch's cap, and porte cochere. The Parkers fashion architectural details from model railroading parts, jewelry findings, and cake decorations. Their mansions are often copies of full-size homes; this one is modeled on a Victorian in Bridgeport, CT.

Marge and Gil Gudgel specialize in building 1/144th scale houses like this plantation house. The 1" scale "For Sale" sign was painted by George Schlosser.

SMALLER MEASURES, GREATER PLEASURES

In small proportions we just beauties see;
And in short measures, life may perfect be

—Ben Johnson

Most miniaturists begin with 1'' scale and work their way down in size. However, standard dollhouse scale would be a great step up for Michigan craftsperson Charles Schmidt who builds 1/144th scale furniture for houses like Plaid Enterprises' MilliMeter Mansion shown here. Plaid no longer produces this line of houses, but Charles continues to build sets of 1/144th scale furniture using 1/32'' basswood and toothpicks. (The 1'' chair shown here for scale is from Collector Miniatures)

Photo by Robert Delgado

Collectors drawn to paper ephemera are often fascinated by the elaborate and whimsical pop-up books and fold-out models popular at the turn of the century. Lew and Barbara Kummerow designed this tiny (1'' x 1/2'') version of a model Pollock's Toy Theater as a kit sure to test the skills of any nimble-fingered do-it-yourselfer. (Photographed courtesy Kummerow Studio of Miniature Design)

In the mid 1970s, Lew and Barbara Kummerow were among the first miniaturists to venture into 1/2'' scale. Beginning with 1/2'' furniture, they branched into home construction with miniatures artisan Jim Marcus. Together, they collaborated on "Little Belle," a three-story Victorian townhouse. The Kummerows' ever-expanding line of smaller scale items includes this three-inch tall, four-room cast metal Victorian.

"Nibble, nibble, little mouse! Who nibbles at my little house?"

—the Brothers Grimm, from "Hansel & Gretel"

*This 1/2" scale house traveled 4000 miles from Washington State to Washington, DC, to appear on the cover of **Nutshell News** in July 1983. This 11-room house built from 1/4" fir plywood shows the detailed construction and finishing effects possible in smaller scales. Builder Clell Boyce of Victorian Times Miniatures modeled his weathered Victorian farmhouse on a full-size home which once stood on the banks of Lacamas Lake in Washington State. The house measures 17"H x 21"W x 12"D. (Collection of Ann Kimball Pipe)*

Photo by Pat Burt Photography

❧ SMALLER MEASURES, GREATER PLEASURES ❧

I'll have a little cabin
All painted white and red
With shutters for the window
And curtains for the bed

—Marchette Chute, My Plan

Judee Williamson works adeptly in both 1'' and 1/2'' scales by applying basic principles of design and color coordination (along with the theatrical panache gleaned from her years as a costume designer) to the creation of her miniature settings. Rather than scale down measurements inch for inch, Judee approaches smaller scale projects with a set designer's eye for proportion, spacial relationships, and movement of the eye from one focal area to another. An unusually high ceiling, reflective surfaces, and dramatic verticals portrayed in the white columns and sofa upholstery, give this small 1/2'' scale room a feeling of additional space. (House owned by Anne Boomer)

Photo by Yvonne Pessel

One delightful aspect of 1/2'' scale is that it fits neatly into spaces where other miniatures might look incongruous. Imagine a smoke shop inside a tobacco tin, or a country kitchen inside a tea kettle — the possibilities can lead to hours of speculation. Joanne Hipple created her 1/4'' scale, sophisticated version of The Old Woman Who Lived in a Shoe inside a ceramic boot. Joanne made the boot and all the tiny furnishings inside.

Photo courtesy Tillie's Tiny Treasures

In all our wandering 'round,
A sight like this we never found

—Palmer Cox, The Brownies in the Toy Shop

While researching **Nutshell News's** July 1982 issue on smaller scales, our staff consistently received two comments from hobbyists reluctant to try smaller scales: 'There aren't enough products available', and 'You can't achieve the degree of realism in 1/2″ or smaller scales that you can in 1″.' We decided to see for ourselves how true these observations were by gathering the products and assembling them into room settings. These three rooms show some of the decorating possibilities we found in smaller scales.

We found that Victorian furnishings were the most prevalent and popular pieces in 1/2″ scale. This room is furnished almost entirely with elaborately carved Belter-style furniture by Susan Gentsch, whose skill refutes the belief that fine detail is unattainable in this smaller size.

Because most miniaturists prefer to recreate the past rather than the present, the demand and availability of modern-style furnishings is less than that of period pieces. However, we found a number of nicely executed contemporary pieces in 1/2″ scale for this casual room centered around Dorothy St. Onge's ''pit grouping'' and rattan pieces from Lovely Little Homes.

Traditional Colonial pieces were also readily available in 1/2″ scale. Fine furnishings and minute turnings don't faze Ted Norton, whose 1/2″ Windsor chairs shown here are tiny works of art. Francis Whittemore's glassware and an upholstered wing chair by Mel Prescott also appear in this room, along with the work of several other miniaturists.

Ah! you are so great, and I am so small,
I tremble to think of you, World; at all

—William Brighty Rands

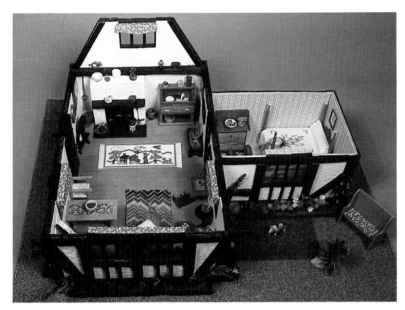

Part of the fun of working with smaller scales is the challenge of finding or making miniatures to complete your setting. Needleworker Nancy Johnson made most of the furniture in this 1/2'' scale Tudor cottage she uses as a display for her 40-mesh needlework. The three-room cottage began as a Tudor Models, Ltd. kit; Nancy added a bedroom and landscaping.

While most of the photographs in this book focus on 1'' scale or smaller objects, there are some larger scale miniatures which, because of their remarkable realism, deserve equal attention. Paul Crees, whose 28'' tall Greta Garbo is shown here, is one of England's hottest doll artists. A former set and costume designer with Britain's Royal Ballet and Royal Shakespeare Company, Paul's dolls are mirror images of stage and screen actresses. He uses latex, plaster of Paris, wax, and soft sculpture to achieve his haunting look-alikes of Marlene Deitrich, Jean Harlow, Joan Crawford, Judy Garland, and others.

Accurately proportioned and realistic-looking dolls and accessories are the most difficult items to find or make in smaller scales. A charcoal portraitist and model railroading buff, Brenda Banghart specializes in making 1/4'' scale miniatures like this housewife encircled by a full-size wedding band. Brenda also makes 1/4'' furniture and accessories.

Photo by Anne D. Smith

The Children's Hour

"Childhood is not from birth to a certain age and at a certain age the child is grown, and puts away childish things," said poet Edna St. Vincent Millay. Rather, "childhood is the kingdom where nobody dies. Nobody that matters, that is." Thus, Alice, Wendy, Peter Pan, Snow White, Little Red Riding Hood, Pinocchio, and a host of other fairy tale characters remain youthful in our memories.

The miniatures world is peopled with full-grown children. Part of the joy of the hobby is that it allows you to remain a child and live out all your fantasies. In the world of miniatures, work even becomes play. Ask a collector what she is doing as she decorates her dollhouse for Christmas and she will reply, "I'm playing." Ask a woodworker what he is doing in his basement workshop at three a.m. making spindles, and he will explain, "I was playing with my new toy — the lathe I got for my birthday."

Over the centuries, miniatures have crossed back and forth through the realm of childhood as Sunday toys, instructional playthings, or simply as entertaining and diverting objects. They have also held a significant place in the world of adult pleasures. Today, miniatures as we know them are once again an adult hobby, a pastime which lets adults indulge themselves in the innocence, whimsy, and imagination of childhood.

Child-related themes crop up often in miniature room settings and vignettes: nurseries, toy shops, play rooms, the pinks and blues of a little girl or boy's bedroom, all hold inexplicable charm. Children themselves, when placed in a setting, add a warm, human touch to a scene and imbue it with life. Whether your 1" scale child sits meekly in a window seat reading a book or romps about the room finger painting the walls and unhinging the furniture, children lend a special spark to any room they enter. Devils or angels, we can't resist them — perhaps because they make us feel young ourselves.

Mighty glad I ain't a girl — ruther be a boy,
Without them sashes, curls, an' things that's worn by Fauntleroy!

—Eugene Field, Jest 'Fore Christmas

These two conscientious baby sitters know it's feeding time for their tiny charge. Dolls made by Tennessee craftsperson Lynn McEntire possess a haunting Old World charm thanks to Lynn's life-long love for antique dolls. A professional caterer, former antiques shop owner, and mother of two, Lynn designs dolls one-half inch to three inches tall, most with swivel heads and moveable limbs.

Children are irrepressible, and the portrait dolls, below, by Joan Blackwood capture the essence of a child's eager, inquisitive nature. Joan thinks of her porcelain dolls as people and sculpts them from clay using a seam ripper. She then makes her own molds. Joan's twin sister Jane Bradbury is also a dollmaker, and Joan credits her twin with introducing her to miniatures.

Photo by Anne D. Smith

Running off with the circus has tempted many a youngster, and these clowns less than one inch tall certainly seem to enjoy life under the Big Top. Texas artisan Bernice Stevens sculpts the delicate figures from porcelain. An avid collector of many things, including porcelain and antique china, Bernice works freehand to create her one-of-a-kind figures.

Photo by Linda Gale

There's a quaint little place they call Lullaby Town —
It's just back of those hills where the sunsets go down

—John Irving Diller, Lullaby Town

Interior designers Barbara DeVilBiss and Patricia Smith joined forces to build a miniature world inside a three foot by eight foot linen closet for a 1982 New Jersey decorators' showhouse project. One of the scenes they duplicated in 1'' scale was this Victorian nursery Barbara had designed earlier in full-size. Characters from Lewis Carol's **Alice In Wonderland** and from Beatrix Potter tales are represented in the room.

Photo courtesy Barbara DeVilBiss

Collecting antique dolls led Margo Gregory to recreate her treasures in miniature. After trying wood and papier mache, she settled on porcelain and now produces dolls of her own design. Her Victorian era dolls come in a number of sizes. The little girl who can't make her puppet work stands six-and-one-half inches tall.

Photo by Kern Thompson

Tim Kummerow came to the miniatures world through his parents who make a variety of 1'' furniture, accessories, and stained glass. Tim concentrates on reproducing classic paintings like Renoir's ``Mother and Child.'' He works in acrylics, painting portraits, still lifes, land and seascapes.

Leave your supper and leave your sleep,
And come with your playfellows into the street

—Come Out To Play

You might have seen Suzanne Marks's larger porcelain clowns and accessories in specialty shops, or her 1'' scale children may have caught your eye at a miniatures show. Suzanne, an artist for 20 years, moves in both creative worlds. This merry scene is a culmination of her efforts. Her husband Ed built the carousel, and Suzanne sculpted the animals and children.

What do children like more than skipping school or staying up late? Sweets! The tempting Fimo candies above are from Lola Originals. To a child, a dish of ice cream smothered in hot fudge, coated with nuts, and topped with whipped cream is heaven. Florida miniaturist Ann Maselli has a bit of the kid in her still, and her Ice Cream Parlor and Sweet Shop would thrill children of any age. Making a black and white tile floor, wire ice cream parlor furniture, and Coca Cola memorabilia, Ann has concocted the sights, smells, and tastes of yesteryear.

The little boys dance, and the little girls run:
If it's bad to have money, it's worse to have none

—Kate Greenaway

Raggedy Ann and Andy are as all-American as apple pie and the Fourth of July. This Raggedies Room is alive with Anns and Andys collected by California miniaturist Betty Martin. As part of her private collection, Betty has assembled a 29-room Dollorama in which each room carries out a theme and is filled with 1″ scale dolls.

When Debi Marion made a porcelain doll as a Christmas gift for her daughter, it was so well received by Debi's miniaturist mother that she then developed a replica of an antique swivel head, ball-jointed doll three-and-one-half inches tall. This little girl with her doll trunk is a 1″ likeness of Debi's daughter Monique.

Photo by Hixson Photography

Michigan miniaturist, craft teacher, and artist Terry Hensen really has two hobbies: miniatures and boating. When Terry, her husband and two children take their vintage Chris Craft cruiser out for an excursion, Terry also takes her miniatures. Her trademark is the expressive clowns and children she sculpts in varying scales.

THE CHILDREN'S HOUR

Higgledy, piggledy! see how they run
Hopperty, popperty! what is the fun?

—Kate Greenaway

For the miniature mother-to-be, or the collector who can't resist nursery items, Shirley Bloomfield's ultimate baby shop is a delight. Filled with all manner of crocheted layette items, clothing, lace trimmed pillows, toys, and decorative items for Baby's room, this shop attests to Shirley's own warm and nuturing personality — she has left nothing out!

Joann Swanson can take a bit of cardboard, glue, and Sculpey and make almost anything. A contributor of do-it-yourself projects to **Nutshell News**, Joann — the mother of three and an active miniaturist and workshop leader since the early 1970s — has plenty of experience with children's toys like these blocks, checker and Ouija boards she designed in 1" scale.

Dollmaker Sonja Breyer modeled this Oriental brother and sister in porcelain and dressed them in their native clothing reminiscent of Walt Disney's ''It's A Small World'' theme.

Photo by Anne D. Smith

Castles Fair
And Far Away

Miniaturists, by nature, have a bit of the dreamer in them. If they didn't, they would never be able to look at other people's castoffs and discover real treasures. Despite what may be happening in the outside world, a miniaturist knows that within the realm of 1'' scale reality, ''happily ever aftering'' is highly possible. Perhaps the miniatures world is an adult version of the Land of Make Believe. In it, we build 1'' scale romanticized versions of full-size settings, perfect the imperfections of life, and arrange the world in a more pleasant and manageable form.

Recall the fairy tales you enjoyed as a child, the castles, kings, knights and ladies, sorcerers and fairies you conjured from the pages of picture books. If you are a bit of a dreamer, it is doubtful that you remember the castle's damp chill, or the hardships of life in those simpler, less comfortable and far from hygienic times.

Instead, you see the towering presence of Camelot, its castle turrets decorated with colorful pennants billowing in the breeze, its gleaming halls, flower-filled meadows, laughing maids and chivalrous knights.

Miniaturists often hark back to an age of romance which, we believe, was characterized by haunting love ballads sung by troubadours, picnics of sweetmeats and heady wine, and jousting tournaments where knights displayed uncommon valor in the name of chivalry. We dream the same dreams King Arthur shared with his knights of the Round Table. And from these dreams come miniature settings which combine fact and fantasy in a regal manner.

To create such settings, some miniaturists immerse themselves in medieval history, learning castle construction techniques, furniture and clothing styles, heating and illumination methods, food preparation, etc. They might even read a bit of Chaucer or play reruns of *Camelot* to evoke the proper mood.

The castle-oriented hobbyist might choose an authentic castle to duplicate in miniature, and more than likely this would be an edifice of English, French, Spanish, Italian or German origin. If the designer decides to keep furnishings true to the period, he or she may have to do some kit bashing or scratch building to duplicate the specific pieces needed. Foods will be less of a challenge, since several miniatures craftspeople have earned their culinary degree in medieval cookery, as well as dishes from other princely periods. Lighting devices will not be too difficult to locate, since a number of artisans already make fixtures in several castle-related styles, and some will also forge specific items at your request.

If yours is an early castle setting, the inhabitants will be dressed in fairly simple garb which you might even stitch yourself. If your lords and ladies hail from the Elizabethan era or the reign of a French Louis, the costumes will be much more elaborate and will require detailed research and skilled sewing techniques. But not to worry, there are many superior miniatures needleartists who are also intrigued by these periods and who can whip up a redingote or farthingale with ultimate ease.

This is beginning to sound like a great deal of work, you say? The purpose was to indulge a flight of fancy, not create an historic monument? Well, fear not, there is a place in the miniature realm for these dreams, also. In fact, castles which spring purely from flights of fantasy have the serendipitous quality of castles remembered from fairy tales. These manors can be built and furnished in any style or mix of styles because they spring from the imagination. One collector has used her castle to incorporate every style and period she has ever enjoyed. Such a grouping wouldn't succeed in a classic Georgian or Colonial two-over-two structure, but it is right at home in her castle.

In essence, castles are meant for dreaming. In them, contradictions of time or place magically disappear. You are the sole ruler in your castle, and whatever edicts you decree for construction, furnishings, and inhabitants will become the law of the land. Let your imagination run free from memories of castles in your childhood to dreams of what your modern-day castle would be. Remember — anything is possible in the Land of Make Believe.

Am I a king, that I should call my own
This splendid ebon throne?

—Henry Wadsworth Longfellow, From My Armchair

Perhaps because our revolutionary forefathers denied us the pomp and splendor of a monarchy, many Americans are fascinated by the trappings of royalty. There are several castle-oriented miniatures groups which focus primarily on these trappings. Some members of these groups let their imaginations run free as they build their own versions of Mad King Ludwig's manor. Others thoroughly research the turreted structures, massive furniture, and colorful characters who made up this chivalrous, romanticized world.

*What better place to begin a journey through the Land of Make Believe than a majestic castle and a stately English manor? Shown above, Sebo Hall is a 21-room manor house designed and built by Michigan craftsperson David Jones in conjunction with collectors Alex and Kate Sebo. The fictional castle dates to the reign of English monarch Henry VIII and measures eight feet by four feet on its landscaped base. The Hall's kitchen is featured elsewhere in this book. Taking the name of her five-story Astolat Castle from Tennyson's **Idylls of the King**, Arizona miniaturist Elaine Diehl has built a massive nine foot tall castle which encompasses under one roof all the designs and styles Elaine has enjoyed over the years.*

Rocks and castles towering high;
Hills and dales and streams and fields;
And knights in armour riding by,
With nodding plumes and shining shields

—Gabriel Setoun, Jack Frost

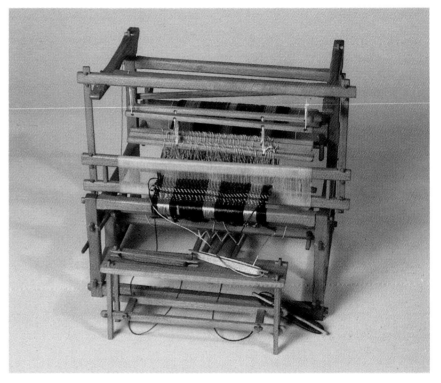

Florida crafter Norma Smithers bought a small scale twenty-five cent child's toy castle at a flea market and then worked her own magic on it. Using hard-drying putties and landscaping materials, she built moats, moss-covered stone walls, and trellised hideaways.

The frequent allusions to spinning and weaving throughout legends and fairy tales attest to the importance of these pursuits often performed by women. The fabrics created on looms like this one built in miniature by Bill Thelen supplied cloth for garments, linens, and other necessities.

English monarchs Henry VIII, Elizabeth I, and Victoria dramatically influenced the politics and tastes of their day. English artisan Ann Parker has influenced doll collecting tastes since 1973. Ann sculpts original masters for her twelve-inch and smaller dolls in plaster of Paris. Helpers then make bodies, wigs and costumes, turning the dolls back to Ann for final painting and inspection.

Photo by Sylvia Hayes

Former landscape architect, pilot and lumber mill owner Ron Stetkewicz started carving small souvenir items in the early 1970s to use up scrap wood from his mill. Later, Ron honed his skills to 1'' scale and developed an extensive list of maritime items. He also makes brass and cast pieces, and these authentic wooden traveling trunks — ideal for moving valuables from a remote castle to a vacation villa by the sea.

*A knyght ther was, and that a worthy man,
That fro the tyme that he first bigan
To riden out, he loved chivalrie*

—Geoffrey Chaucer, A Perfect Knight

The land of enchantment wouldn't be complete without a wizard to cast spells and mix magic potions. This unique two-story ceramic wizard's den with resident sorcerer was made by Caryn King.

Photo by Ron Stetkewicz

Marie Antoinette's life as queen of France would rival the drama of a modern romance novel. Louisiana doll maker Rosemary Tucker, a professional entertainer for twenty years, understands drama and uses it in sewing costumes for her 1'' scale dolls like this rendition of Marie Antoinette dressed in regal purple.

No proper castle would be complete without its inhabitants' coat of arms. This crest, designed in jest by David Jones for Sebo Hall (shown elsewhere in this book), depicts the owners' interests and lineage.

Photo courtesy David Jones

Mousie, mousie,
Where is your little wee housie?
—Rose Fyleman, Conversation

Jean Kelly, a miniaturist, crafts designer and author for **Nutshell News** and **McCalls Needlework and Crafts** magazines, began this Tudor bedroom with a half-canopied bed by Judee Williamson. Around it she created the chambers of Henry VIII's fictional seventh wife Jocelynde. The tower room — which represented a stylistic departure from Colonial to Tudor when Jean built it in 1978 — includes coffers overflowing with jewels and coins.

Photo by Monte Kelly

Suzanne Loftus-Brigham knows that in the Land of Make Believe, even a mouse can become a Beefeater, Bobbie, or King! A former theatrical and television designer with an obvious sense of whimsy, Suzanne dresses her poseable six- to eight-inch tall mice in period costumes.

In ancient times, a warrior's armor was often a good defense, despite its bulkiness and weight. Ray Sherwood tooled this replica of a Roman centurion's armor and sword from silver.

I dreamt that I dwelt in marble halls,
With vassals and serfs at my side

—Alfred Bunn, Bohemian Girl: Song

A castle or baronial manor requires elaborate and ingenious furnishings. The skills needed to build such furniture come naturally to artisans Judy Shellhaas and Susanne Russo. Judy, whose primary tool is an X-Acto knife, loves precision woodworking and focuses on highly carved Victorian pieces like the pier table and Roman Revival chair, below. Susanne Russo, who began her miniatures career sculpting nudes, quickly established a dual reputation as a builder of inventive furniture. The carved dressing table and chair with swan motif, left, are Susanne's original designs.

Imaginary knights and ladies dance to English madrigals in this four-foot tall stained glass castle built by Jim Kunkel. The electrified structured was originally designed as a jewelry case.

Photo by Anne D. Smith

The splendor falls on castle walls
And snowy summits old in story

—Alfred, Lord Tennyson, Bugle Song

Over the years, Skip Wallon has indulged his love of fantasy by working for Walt Disney World and the Ringling Brothers, Barnum and Bailey Circus World Showcase. He was also part of the creative effort that made the 1'' White House possible. Skip let his imagination run free in building this 1/4'' scale castle and the accompanying Neo-Gothic furniture and lyre clock.

Nothing can be truer than fairy wisdom.
It is as true as sunbeams

—Douglas Jerrold, Fairies

The fanciful little folk who breathe life and laughter into fairy tales, rhymes and legends are an integral part of the Land of Make Believe. What would that magical land be without a few mischievous mice, an elegant rabbit, a dapper pig, a gaggle of clowns, or a forest filled with fairies?

Imagine this dignified ''Marotte'' entertaining at a royal court ball. The full-size ca. 1860 German doll was indeed an entertainment device. Encased in the body is a music box which plays when the doll is swung by its wooden handle. It was used either for adult entertainments or as a christening toy.

A more motley crew of performers you're not likely to see unless the circus comes to town! In fact, Coleen Cantu's belly dancer, fat lady and snake charmer came straight from the Big Top. Other dolls by Bonnie Franklin, Cathy Hansen, and Jean Pardina go along for the ride on the swan carousel seat by Jan and Paul Sanchez.

The Land of Make Believe wouldn't be complete without a few clever and gifted mice, and this ca. 1910 six-piece Viennese bronze mouse band could charm even the most discriminating audience. (Blauer Collection)

Photo by Ellen Krucker Blauer

And now they throng the moonlight glade,
Above — below — on every side,
Their little minim forms arrayed,
In the tricksy pomp of fairy pride
—Joseph Rodman Drake, The Assembling of the Fays

The hunch-backed, hook-nosed and devious Punchinello emerged from the 16th century Commedia Dell'arte and has survived in various forms, including the infamous British cartoon character Punch. These 1'' bisque figures made by Carolyn Robbins are copies of original full-size bisque Punchinellos. (Blauer Collection)

Photo by Ellen Krucker Blauer

She could have danced right out of a Busby Berkley production number in her high-stepping red heels and Big Apple attire. Instead, this jointed all-porcelain 1'' scale beauty is doll artist Sylvia Lyons' tribute to Manhattan, and her contribution to the 1982 IGMA auction of miniatures.

Clown, fool, jester, Harlequin, Punchinello, or Pierrot — whatever he is called, he came of age in the Commedia Dell'arte in the 1500s and has thrived ever since. These harlequins with their French tricorns were made by Paula Watkins. She painted Lawbre's wagon kit and modified its interior into living quarters and dressing room for these traveling entertainers.

With swords of tin and guns of wood,
They wheeled about,
and marched or stood

—Palmer Cox, The Brownies in the Toy Shop

Mermaids have lured sailors toward the rocks in legend and verse since ancient times. This fanciful marine maiden was captured in 1'' scale by Canadian doll artist Joy Parker who, along with husband Wayne, runs a thriving doll business called Swallowhill Doll Dimensions.

In the American colonies, governor's palaces replaced castles, and royal pomp and ceremony gave way to the revolutionary rat-a-tat-tat of the fife and drum corps. Artist Therese Bahl focuses on Colonial themes in her full-size art work and started doing the same in 1'' scale in 1978. These gentlemen are miniature versions of dummy boards, or silent companions — one-dimensional portraits used to decorate the 18th century home.

The Atlanta Toy Museum is a delightful repository of antique dolls, toys and miniatures, with one display devoted to parlor toys — those mechanical marvels which captivated the family's attention before the advent of radio and television. These German and French automata encompass a number of jesters and musicians including the long-legged youth serenading the moon.

Photo by Kern Thompson

Fairies, black, grey, green, and white,
You moonshine revellers, and shades of night
—Shakespeare, Merry Wives of Windsor

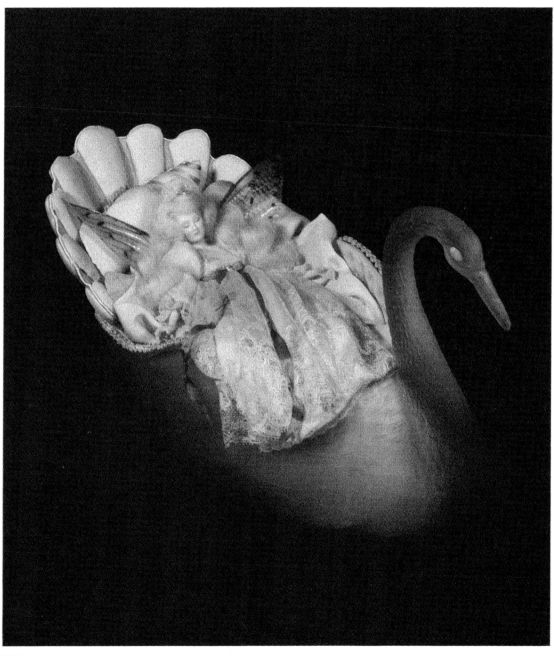

This lovely princess nestled in a crystal swan bower is worlds away in the Land of Nod. Nancy Wickersham transformed the antique crystal swan container into an exquisite bed. To heighten the iridescent effect, she gave the swan opal eyes. The shell-shaped pillows have real sea shells as forms. Sylvia Mobley made the porcelain princess and Nancy dressed her.

Photo by Ann Ruble

The city mouse lives in a house;—
The garden mouse lives in a bower

—Christina Rossetti, The City Mouse

Beatrix Potter's children's stories firmly established mice as upstanding citizens in Storybook Land. Dee Snyder also finds these whiskered creatures adorable, and her Harvest Home wreath creates a cozy environment reminiscent of The Borrowers for this happy family. Designed as an exploded view of a mouse nest in a corn field, the scene was inspired by watercolors in Jill Barklem's Brambly Hedge series of children's books. Incorporated in the scene are real nuts, berries and grains as well as dried herbs, spices and potpourri which add fragrance, texture, and visual interest. Miniaturist and fellow mouse lover Bunnie Ward dressed the mice.

Photo by Dee Snyder

They think of their homes and manors there,
Their gentle spouses and damsels fair
—The Chanson de Roland

In a land where fantasy reigns supreme, teddy bears are as likely to enjoy a picnic as you or I. The "beary" human antics of this furry group were conceived by Kathryn Franze and Susan Johnson, makers of 1" scale jointed Tig-gyWinkles bears. Roberta Partridge concocted the sweet treats for the outing.

Photo by Jill Riner

There was an old woman who lived in a shoe,
She had so many children she didn't know what to do
—The Old Woman

Every child has his or her favorite nursery rhyme, fairy tale, or bedtime story. We often carry these memories into adulthood and read those same beloved tales to our children. Children's literature is a collecting genre in itself, and one which often attracts miniaturists. Many of us seem instinctively drawn to the gentle, whimsical, and imaginative nature of these tales which offer so many possibilities for recreation in miniature.

The children's rhyme about the old woman who lived in a shoe is especially pertinent to miniaturists. The implications of a smaller than life-size environment are just waiting for a creative hobbyist to put them in physical form. Two variations on the theme are pictured here.

Jackie Transue's version of "The Old Woman Who Lived In A Shoe" was fashioned from Super Sculpey and stands less than two inches tall! Jackie also makes porcelain dolls.

Multi-talented artisan Dana Pyle used a full-size lace up boot as the base of his version of "The Old Woman Who Lived In A Shoe." He added a roof and two bays, landscaped the setting, and included not only the Old Woman and her many offspring, but also a hillside for Jack and Jill, a barnyard for Little Boy Blue, a wall for Humpty Dumpty, and a garden for Mary, Mary.

The King was in the counting house,
Counting out his money;
The Queen was in the parlor,
Eating bread and honey

Since they began making miniatures in 1980, Stephanie Blythe and Susan Snodgrass have taken a unique approach to their work. Susan, a former student of acting and theater design who later designed clothing and jewelry in Manhattan, and Stephanie, a fabric designer and illustrator, are known for their 1" scale fairy domes. Inspirations for their work often come from literature or classic films. Here, in an early setting made by the pair, the Queen of Hearts (made by Sylvia Mobley) notices that the Knave has run off with her tarts.

Photo courtesy
Stephanie Blythe and Susan Snodgrass

Scarlett O'Hara, heroine of Margaret Mitchell's epic **Gone With The Wind**, is dressed for the Twelve Oaks barbecue. Behind her stands Tara, built in 1" scale by 22-year-old New Yorker Ronnie Gatto. A student at Parsons School of Design, Ronnie has built miniatures since he was 12. It took him two years to complete his Tara — a 17-room plantation house measuring seven-and-one-half feet long by three feet high. Using the novel and other books about the movie — and by watching the film countless times — Ronnie created what he feels is the most detailed scale version of Tara ever attempted.

Photo by Terry Yacona

Its streets are of silver, its buildings of gold,
And its palaces dazzling things to behold

—John Irving Diller, Lullaby Town

Every successful miniature setting tells a tale. To honor the greatest storyteller of all time, California miniaturist Madelyn Cook built a lavish sultan's chambers where Scheherazade weaves her tales of 1001 Arabian Nights. The room with its sunken pool combines Indian and Arabian influences. Much of the interior was built from a shesham wood inlaid tray. Throughout, Madelyn used wood, brass and jewelry castoffs to contrive scenes from the tales. Galia Bazylko made the sultan and Scheherazade.

Photo by Jim Cook

Sherlock Holmes' fictional adventures have long held fascination for a coterie of mystery buffs. In the miniatures world, members of the Mini-Tonga Scion Society devote themselves to collecting 1'' scale Holmes memorabilia. Here, Dee Snyder, a founding member of the Society, has assembled her version of a modern Sherlockian's bachelor pad. The gentleman, a member of the Mini-Tongas, displays a miniature 221B Baker Street room on his mantel. Bookshelves contain a collection of leather bound Holmes volumes, a television plays a Basil Rathbone movie, and other Sherlockian items abound.

Photo by Dee Snyder

*She walks in beauty like the night
Of cloudless climes and starry skies;
And all that's best of dark and bright
Meets in her aspect and her eyes*

—Lord Byron, She Walks in Beauty

Canadian miniaturist Wendy Russell designed this 1'' version of Miss Haversham's wedding banquet from Charles Dickens' novel **Great Expectations**. The room was built by James Molnar, and to it Wendy has added a collection of found objects including fish hook candlesticks and an apple head doll dressed in 100-year-old lace. To give the room the appropriate look of decay, Wendy scattered the contents of a vacuum cleaner bag over the scene.

It's difficult to imagine that a princess sleeping on such a bed could feel a tiny pea under the mattress, but so goes the story. In Nancy Wickersham's version of the tale, there are 13 hand-dyed ''eiderdown'' coverlets of velvet, crepe de chine and silk, all decorated with embroidery and antique laces. Nancy also carved and gold-leafed the bed . . . and tucked a pea beneath the bedding!

I will make a palace fit for you and me
Of green days in forests and blue days at sea
—Robert Louis Stevenson, I Will Make You Brooches

Hollywood — the ultimate Land of Make Believe. For the 1982 ''Hollywood — The Golden Years'' NAME National Houseparty miniaturists Eve Karoblis and Ed Mabe recreated Stage 27 on MGM's Main Lot where ''The Wizard of Oz'' was filmed. The 1'' scale set within a set depicts two scenes from the movie — Dorothy's bedroom and the Bad Witch's aerie. The sound stage's high ceilings allow fly space for additional scenery and scaffolding for lights and cameras. Brooms and saw horses attest to the less glamorous work of movie making.

Woodcarver Frances Armstrong's minute miniatures elicit awe from hobbyists whose discipline and attention to detail are less than this talented Canadian's. Shown here is Frances' 1/144th scale rendition of the Fantasy Island manor house completed in natural woods.

Celebrations
Through The Year

The celebration of traditions brings a sense of balance and stability to the shape of man's days. No matter how simple or elaborate, how obscure or documented these traditions may be, their observance gives the participant a sense of belonging to something permanent. Man instinctively senses the importance of these rituals, and celebrates them with friends and family gathered round.

Traditional celebrations vary according to the observers' nationality or region, age, education, and station in life. Many traditions and the celebrations which spring from them are rooted in a religious background. Ironically, these religious celebrations often borrow liberally from their pagan predecessors. After the Romans invaded England in 43 A.D, they banned the observance of all pagan holidays and the worship of pagan gods. When their British subjects ignored these edicts, the Romans compromised, incorporating aspects of select pagan traditions and holidays into the Christian ritual.

Some of the most revered traditions and celebrations are those whose origins are ancient and often obscure. It is fascinating to realize, when we hang mistletoe at Christmas, toss rice at newlyweds, pass out treats on Halloween, or send a Valentine to a sweetheart, that we are performing rituals which are hundreds, even thousands of years old. Such practices handed from generation to generation impart a deep and moving sense of

universal time and man's place within this dimension. Certainly, a race without traditions and celebrations would be a joyless one.

Specific holidays have often been the source of specific rituals. Christmas is among the most ritual-laden holidays of all. While most of us embrace some similar observances of the Christmas season, each family and individual establishes his or her personal means of celebration. These private observances are the most cherished traditions of all.

Christmas is a particulary important time at our house. The Christmas baking begins weeks in advance, allowing ample time for the traditional fruitcake to "age." The list of holiday treats remains essentially the same year to year, and woe to the cook if she should neglect someone's favorite treat! The same cherished ornaments have decorated the tree for years — some dating back almost 30 seasons. Thanks to the decorations and holiday spirit, the entire house takes on a glow and seems to wrap everyone who enters in its comforting warmth.

In essence, holiday celebrations are meant for the young and old, for the religious and secular by nature. The primary ingredients of any traditional holiday celebration are good company, good food and good cheer. When these elements are present, any celebration is sure to bring enjoyment, a sense of community, and a richer meaning to the holiday being honored.

Heap on more wood,
The wind is chill;
But let it whistle as it will,
We'll keep our Christmas merry still!

—Sir Walter Scott

Poor tired Santa! The Christmas rush is almost at an end — just a few more Noah's Arks to paint and it's off in the sleigh on his midnight rounds. He and his elves catch a few winks in the midst of this busiest night of the year. Mary Penet sculpted this Santa and her husband Phil Levigne painted him.

Photo courtesy Phil Levigne and Mary Penet

What better time of year to begin our tribute to holidays than the festive Christmas season? For many of us, this time of year means visiting friends and relatives who open wide the door of hospitality. Busy elves have left their Christmas cheer at this inviting door with its apple and pineapple wreaths and boxwood kissing ball. The decorations reminiscent of those seen in Colonial Williamsburg were designed by Nancy Ranney.

Photo by Shelby Harris

All paths lead to you
Where e'er I stray,
You are the evening star
At the end of day

—Blanche Shoemaker Wagstaff, All Paths Lead to You

Everything's coming up Valentines in this sweetheart room by interior designer Mary Ester Marsac and her husband John. Cupids dance around the gilt-framed mirror, love letters lie on the desk, a love bird croons from her cage, and a guitar stands ready to play romantic tunes.

Photo by Christopher Robin Fluke

The beauty of this ornately decorated church would lend an aura of pageantry to any religious celebration. Built in the 1930s by a retired German cabinetmaker, the church is believed to be a replica of St. Vincent's Catholic Church in Los Angeles, CA. The builder skillfully combined varying shades of wood for the interior's rich patina. The building measures forty-one inches high by sixty-three inches long by twenty-eight-and-one-half inches wide and took the maker seven years to build.

Holidays are Ann Maselli's favorite times of year. Her sense of fun and good cheer shines through every miniatures project she tackles, from domes to rooms to accessory items. Creator of **Nutshell News's** ''Dome of the Month'' and ''Room of the Month'' how-to series, Ann has a flair for customizing pieces like this Chrysnbon hutch and using modeling clay, jewelry findings, and castoffs to create realistic-looking accessories at bargain prices.

Photo by Ann Maselli

Say thou lov'st me while thou live,
I to thee my love will give
—Love Me Little, Love Me Long

Although Valentines have been sent and received for centuries, the Victorians developed the custom to a high art. This elegant — and slightly fickle — young lady by Susan Sirkis pens thank yous to the beaux who have showered her with chocolates and cards. The lace and mother of pearl fan and full-size Valentines serving as a backdrop are authentic Victorian pieces. The lady's writing desk and chair were made by Larry Worthington and were decorated by Jean Jakeway.

Photo by Jill Riner

Twenty-five years of marriage definitely calls for a celebration, and this couple plans on spending it quietly with a few close friends. The New York penthouse setting was created by the husband and wife team of Phil Levigne and Mary Penet. They made or modified everything in the room and sculpted the dolls as well.

Photo courtesy Phil Levigne and Mary Penet

*I believe love, pure and true,
Is to the soul a sweet, immortal dew*

—Mary Ashley Townsend, Creed

Here comes Peter Cotton Tail — on the trail down a mountain of jellybeans! These irresistibly furry bunnies were created by Joann Swanson.

Knotts Berry Farm in Buena Park, CA has the distinction of housing a unique miniatures collection amassed over several decades by the Mott family, founders of NAME. The collection includes rare individual miniature objects, room settings and antiques. Shown here is a gala wedding reception peopled by antique dolls.

This double wedding ceremony is pure bliss — perhaps because it takes place on a street lined with lithographed paper on wood houses manufactured by the R. Bliss Manufacturing Company in the 19th century. The scene depicts Marthasville — the early name for Atlanta — and is part of a display of Bliss houses in the Atlanta Doll and Toy Museum. The dolls were dressed by contemporary doll artisan Margo Gregory.

Photo by Kern Thompson

Jack-o'-lanterns grinning
Shadows on a screen
Shrieks and starts and laughter —
This is Halloween!

—Dorothy Brown Thompson, This Is Halloween

Despite the evil reputation of witches, it's doubtful that homely witch Karla has wicked intentions. Her maker Joan Haigh says Karla has the face only a mother could love. Many of Joan's 1'' scale figures sculpted either in Fimo or porcelain have distinctive personalities.

Photo by Jeanne Sellers

Mary Hinckley's sense of humor and her admiration for Charles Addams' cartoons in **The New Yorker** led her to create her wacky and wonderful Addams' Family House. The three-story structure with rooms sixteen inches deep was built by Mary's son Jack in 1973. The project won Mary a blue ribbon at the 1978 Tiny Treasures Society show in Boston. A bed of nails, man-eating plant, noose swing, and a miniature version of Hairy Cousin ''It'' lend macabre charm to this eery abode peopled by Morticia, Gomez, Lurch and the rest.

Photo by Ron Bergeron

Diminutive Diversions

In my career as editor of **Nutshell News**, I have taken great delight in the reaction from non-miniaturists when they discover what the magazine is all about. While they may not be adult collectors, many admit to enjoying a dollhouse as a child. Some have seen or read about a miniatures exhibit, and others know someone who owns a dollhouse.

I have also had the pleasure of discovering that there are thousands of collecting hobbies which occupy people's time, energy, and finances, and give them great joy. From buttons to old bottles, circus memorabilia to antique automobiles, collecting is a hobby for hundreds of thousands of Americans.

There is a theory that an interest in collecting is something you are born with, not something you acquire over time. I'm not completely convinced of that, because I myself am a bit of a hybrid collector. Collecting was "in my blood" through inheritance, but I didn't actively pursue it until I became associated with miniatures. Now my hobby is collecting, and I have become just as avid as the next person when it comes to the specific items I collect.

A hobby can be defined as any activity done outside your nine-to-five routine which gives you pleasure. I think pleasure is the key word here. Whether you paint, play an instrument, forge fine jewelry, refurbish antique cars, or write science fiction thrillers, you do it primarily for the pleasure and sense of accomplishment the activity gives you. If, somewhere along the way, you make a little money doing what you enjoy, you have achieved the best of both worlds.

The pursuit of miniatures as a hobby is particularly fascinating and challenging because the hobby's essence is recreating the full-size world in 1'' scale. Consequently, a miniaturist can be a designer, decorator, builder, electrician, fine wood carver, painter, seamstress, metalsmith, potter, sculptor — the list is almost endless. This far-reaching range of creativity means the hobbyist need never be bored. In addition to the diversity of craft areas incorporated in miniature making and collecting, the amount of social history the miniaturist digests in the course of research on any project is immense.

Could I be suggesting that miniatures are the universal hobby? Far be it from me to draw such conclusions — afterall, I'm a bit prejudiced! This chapter, however, is a tribute to the diversity of the hobby. On these pages, you will find 1'' versions of sporting activities, needlearts, jewelry making, porcelain sculpting and pottery, musical pastimes, woodworking, and many other fine art and handcrafts. There is even a miniature version of a miniaturist's workshop!

> *For when the One Great Scorer comes*
> *To write against your name,*
> *He marks — not that you won or lost —*
> *But how you played the game*
>
> —Sir Joshua Reynolds, Alumnus Football

Every hobby requires tools, and Howard Chambers, a crafter of 1'' scale objects for 15 years, has included every tool the miniaturist could want in his version of the ideal hobby workshop.

Photo by Howard Chambers

Riding, showing, breeding, and caring for horses is a hobby which becomes a passion and a career for some aficionados. Former librarian Sylvia Rountree is one such equestrienne who turned her passion to profit by establishing the Dolls' Cobbler, specialist in leather horse-related goods for miniaturists. Shown here are three versions of her hand-tooled leather side saddle.

Photo by Anne D. Smith

Grandpa has taken his rod and reel down to the old fishin' hole to spend a peaceful afternoon. Fashioned from Sculpey with a wire armature that makes them poseable, all Glenda Hooker's black dolls depict very human — and very lovable — traits.

129

Where your treasure is, there will your heart be also

—St. Matthew, The Bible

When two avid collectors share the same house but not the same collecting interests, the problem of how to display their treasures becomes a serious concern. California craftsperson Madelyn Cook has the perfect solution: devote a room to each collector and connect them with a stairway. The blue room shown, right, is filled with china and porcelain by Marie Friedman and Frances Steak with some pieces contrived by Madelyn.

The "his" portion of the duo, left, holds a collection of Southwestern and Indian items including kachinas by Marcy and baskets by Edna Olsen. Most of the furniture in the two rooms was made by Madelyn Cook.

Today's home entertainment center requires a pin ball machine, personal computer, portable radio/cassette player, and a credenza for storing computer games and cassettes. If competition gets hot, the smoke alarm will sound a warning, and the air conditioner can cool down the opponents. Teri's Mini Workshop features the pin ball machine. All other items are from Molly Brody Miniatures.

*There is nothing which has yet been contrived by man,
by which so much happiness is produced
as by a good tavern or inn*

—Ben Johnson

This elegant game room is reminiscent of an upper-crust English Tudor-style tavern, with its English print wallpaper and timbered ceiling. There are areas for billiards, chess, and poker, and refreshments stand ready for the end of any game. This room was designed and built by David Jones for Sebo Hall, shown elsewhere in this book.

The sound of rolling dice or a triumphant call of ``Checkmate!'' was a clear indication that a pleasant evening had begun in a Colonial tavern. This 18th century gentleman and lady in the midst of a chess game were sculpted in porcelain by Baltimore doll artist Deidra Spann.

On a Sunday afternoon in 1910, croquet was often the sport of choice. Drafting and design work with Lockheed gave Jan Riggs the patience to deal with tiny things like her 1'' porcelain Gibson Girl.

131

❧ DIMUNITIVE DIVERSIONS ❧

There I keep my treasures in a box —
Shells and colored glass and queer-shaped rocks,
In a secret hiding place I've made

—Margaret Widdemer, The Secret Cavern

American Indians draw inspiration and materials for their handcrafts from nature. These authentic Indian items by Sal'e-Jo Eaton include pottery, a sand painting, kachina, battle shield, cowboy hat with turquoise decoration, and a deer hide pictograph.

In the late 1970s, Jim Clark bought a $25 potter's wheel as a gift for his wife. When she didn't show interest, Jim used the wheel himself. The rest is the tale of Your Local (full-size) Potter. Eventually, Jim miniaturized his work to the porcelain pieces shown.

Porcelain works by Laurel Coulon aren't easy to come by because this artisan works only when inspired, but her pieces are well worth the search. Using porcelain slip, she builds incredibly thin layers of clay to achieve her minute works of art like this fairy tale coach and team.

The China Room in Maynard Manor, the 42-room mansion assembled by John and Ellen Blauer, boasts many exquisite miniature versions of classic pieces such as Limoges, Capodimonte, and Dresden china.

Photo by Ellen Krucker Blauer

Malcolm Fatzer has been making unusual handblown miniature glassware since the late 1970s, concentrating on swirling shapes and intriguing overlays of color.

The Chinese plate looked very blue,
And wailed, ''Oh, dear! what shall we do!''
—Eugene Field, The Duel

Until 1977, Carolyn Nygren Curran was a full-size production potter. Now she specializes in historically researched miniature pots, preferably those originally thrown in the Northeast. She concentrates on utilitarian wheel-thrown forms one would find in the 17th and 18th century kitchen. Shown here are Carolyn's versions of 18th century salt-glazed stoneware.

The glitter of the Victorian gas light era comes to life when a visitor enters the California home of miniaturists Len and Kathy Schiada. The couple has decorated their home in Gay Nineties antiques, and they also recreate 1'' scale light fixtures from this period. Many of their creations like this six-arm fixture are reproductions of pieces from historic Western mansions and hotels of the period.

Robert Olszewski's name is synonymous with fine miniature sculpting. Bob's 1'' ''Dancer'' was one of his first lost wax sculptures.

A vastly different style of decorative pottery is made by the Pueblo Indians who use earth tone dyes for the elaborate detailing of their stoneware. The Spanish armoire which holds these pieces was made by Elena Lamb.

This rococo-style ceramic punch bowl with cups and cherub candlesticks is a Victorian's delight. The pieces were made by Paul McNeely. Ferd Sobel made the sideboard.

> A *million little diamonds*
> Twinkled on the trees;
> And all the little children cried,
> "A jewel, if you please!"
> —Winter Jewels

Former television set designer Elmer Tag and his wife Jean, a teacher, are devoted to promoting miniatures as an art form. These hand thrown and sculpted porcelain pieces were made by Jean.

Phyllis Tucker is well known in the miniatures world for her elegant crystal chandeliers which add sparkle and magic to any setting they grace. "Adriene," with its twelve individual lights, was her first multi-lit piece and was made from 3mm faceted Austrian crystals and handmade gold chain.

During the late 1970s, Gerry Rynders, one of Canada's most skilled scientific glassblowers, turned his science to art with the creation of chandeliers like this eight-tiered electrified piece above made of over 700 tiny glass beads.

A self-taught miniaturist and the wife of a Methodist minister, Barbara Bunce began making 1" scale dressed beds over 12 years ago. She more recently added beautifully detailed and perfectly scaled mini jewelery to her repertoire.

Photo by Anne D. Smith

Arizona sculptor Jim Pounder studies the musculature of his subjects before recreating them in bronze. Most of his miniature sculptures, like this Crow Chief, concentrate on Western themes.

And this shall be for music when no one else is near,
The fine song for singing, the rare song to hear!
—Robert Louis Stevenson, I Will Make You Brooches

The music room in Jack and Shirley Bloomfield's nine-room mansion modeled after Tara includes work by many noted artisans and has been the scene of numerous elegant Southern soirees. Scarlett and Rhett were sculpted in porcelain by Marty Saunders.

The name Ralph Partelow, Jr., has become synonymous over the past seven years with top quality miniature keyboard instruments, particularly pianos. Ralph, a Christian minister and missionary, has built pianos as a hobby since his childhood when a love for classical music and the piano led him to correspond with John Steinway of Steinway piano manufacturing fame. This concert grand is a classic example of Ralph's artistry.

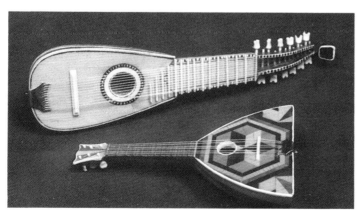

Canadian woodworker Ken Manning is captivated by the beauty and craftsmanship found in early musical instruments like this Balalaika and Mandora, and he recreates this fine art in miniature.

Sheila Kwartler began making miniature dolls in the late 1970s and has quickly risen to the top of her field, both in 1'' scale and larger doll design. Her Jou-Jou de la Chambre, an articulated porcelain can-can dancer is, Sheila says, ''authentically dressed'' in the split pantaloons worn by true French cabaret dancers.

*There is sweet music here that softer falls
Than petals from blown roses on the grass*

—Alfred, Lord Tennyson, Choric Song

Delia Reynolds and her son Michael made beautiful music as a miniatures team when they combined their crafting and collecting skills to assemble this French Baroque Music Room inspired by scenes from Versailles. Michael made most of the furniture in the room, and Delia created the chandelier.

Strike up the band! These miniature brass horns would add a resounding musical note to any diminutive conservatory. (Blauer Collection)

Doll artist Angela Dickens based this miniature setting of a French family musicale on a full-size painting in the Louvre, Paris. The men play instruments while the ladies sing in accompaniment.

We are the music-makers
And we are the dreamers of dreams

—Arthur O'Shaughnessy, Ode

A music room of a slightly different tone is this record producer's office filled with the latest state-of-the-art sound gear. Tape decks, stereo and video equipment, and other furnishings were made by Joen Ellen Kanze as a tribute to her son who is in the recording business.

Accomplished needleartist Deanna Von Drake has won numerous awards and national recognition for her full-size needlework. She specializes in authentic reproductions of 18th century pieces like this needlework painting of Boston Common in 1'' scale.

Barbara Caverly's graceful porcelain ballerina is captured en pointe in a lilting arabesque. Except for her head, the doll was cast as one continuous piece and her tutu is made of 18 layers of illusion netting.

Photo by Barbara Caverly

After a busy day of sewing, the industrious and tidy Shaker ladies stored their yard goods away in pieces like this Shaker sewing chest. New England miniaturist Paul Rouleau scaled this 1'' chest down from a full-size piece.

The boxes come out
From closets and chests,
With odd sorts of clothes
Like old hats and vests

—Dorothy Brown Thompson, I Like Housecleaning

Needleartist Sharon Garmize has the sharpest eyes in the business when it comes to working on fine 40 to 84 mesh silk gauze canvas. She has won numerous awards for her needlework, including The Princess Grace Award bestowed on her in Monaco. Sharon uses a No. 15 beading needle in her work on pieces such as this 18th century Persian Herez carpet.

Photo by Sarah Salisbury

This gauzy, beribboned negligee fit for a princess was stitched by Irene Thursland. Note the many silk rosettes which decorate the gown.

Photo by Susan Sirkis

This 1″ embroiderer was sculpted by 75-year-old Dilwyn Thomas, a former artist with the Cleveland Museum of Natural History. He builds thin layers of wood putty over wire armature to simulate bone and muscle.

Rosemary Tucker's millinery spans all periods and styles. These 18th century ladies are ready for an afternoon promenade.

Knitting still, knitting still,
Always knitting with a will

Susan Sirkis is an accomplished seamstress and an expert on period clothing. In her ''Small Belongings of Dress'' series in **Nutshell News**, she has given enlightening and anecdotal background notes on historic costumes like this elaborately trained, swagged and pleated 1877 promenade gown made of taupe and gray striped silk.

Mitzi Van Horn has been making miniatures since the 1950s, and her enthusiasm, talent, and quick wit have generated many sparks in the miniatures world ever since. A skilled craftsperson who is equally comfortable wielding a lathe or needle, Mitzi built this chair and also did the needlepoint upholstery.

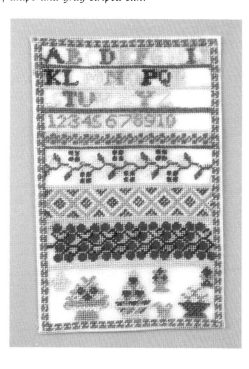

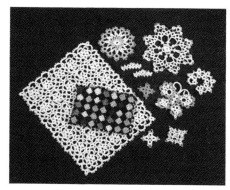

Tatted accessories proliferated in the 19th century. Julie Felzien takes us back to that era with her wide assortment of miniature tatting made from silk and cotton threads.

❧ DIMUNITIVE DIVERSIONS ❦

What do you weave, O ye flower-girls
With tassels of azure and red?

—Sarojini Naidu, In the Bazaars of Nyderabad

Former cabinetmaker and long-time miniaturist Leon Scott has developed a special
technique for the tufting on his furniture.
Shown here is his watered silk Chippendale
sofa.

Photo by Marie Friedman

For her authentic miniature rag rugs, Mona
Crucitti uses a method of weaving thin fabric
strips together which packs them down to perfect
scale. The overshot coverlet on the bed is Mona's
scaled down version of a Colonial original.

As miniatures collector Esther Robertson encouraged her son
Bill to perfect his 1″ scale building talents, she honed her
own skills as a needleworker. Bill hand carved this tilt top
table from Swiss pear wood, and Esther did the petit point in-
set based on an Italian painting on 60 mesh silk gauze.

❧ DIMUNITIVE DIVERSIONS ❧

A *picture is a poem without words*
—Horace

Photo by Carol Tabas

Joan Carson and Jim McNee incorporated living plants into their 1'' scale Courtyard setting displayed at the 1981 Philadelphia Flower Show whose theme was ''A Place of Leisure.'' In the courtyard between a needlearts store and a frame shop, members of an amateur art class have set up their easels to paint outdoors.

Californian Robin Tyler uses oils for her miniature canvases and takes her inspirations from the Impressionists and John Singer Sargent, many of whose works she has duplicated in 1'' scale.

Catherine Last scales down her knowledge of painted faux finishes to create dazzling effects on miniatures such as these wooden accessories turned by David Krupick and Brandt Keys. A student of the late painter Isabel O'Neil, author of the book **The Art of the Painted Finish for Furniture and Decoration**, Cathy added her magic touch to these pieces to create a faux malachite finish.

Photo by Max Andrews

Oh, there is a little artist
Who paints in the cold night hours
Pictures for wee, wee children,
Of wondrous trees and flowers
—The Little Artist

Photo by Susan Sirkis

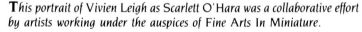

This portrait of Vivien Leigh as Scarlett O'Hara was a collaborative effort by artists working under the auspices of Fine Arts In Miniature.

Marjorie Adams likes to replicate the works of famous painters in oils. This painting by Marjorie, above right, is in the style of English portraitist Thomas Gainsborough.

Donna Gibson and Dianne Donegan have developed a thriving art gallery since they began painting and framing 1'' scale art work in the late 1970s. Dianne is skilled at achieving depths of color in her miniature paintings. Although she works in a number of period styles, she does not duplicate from existing paintings. Donna researches period paintings and frames all Dianne's pieces.

ᘺᕯ DIMUNITIVE DIVERSIONS ᕡᕬ

So sweet the plum trees smell!
Would that the brush that paints the flower
Could paint the scent as well

—Ranko, Plum Trees

Russian-born painter Natasha Beshenkovski draws on a rich heritage of folk art to execute gaily painted and richly detailed pieces like this ``kas'' or European armoire.

Whether the canvas is meant to hang on a wall or lie on the floor, the artistry is the same. Ione Van Beckum ``paints'' miniature rugs on cotton velvet using a rainbow of over 100 waterproof marking pens. To assure even shading, she applies the color in tiny dot strokes. She uses no graphs, charts or preliminary drawings, preferring to paint freehand, even on pieces as complex as this Oriental dragon rug.

Photo by Sarah Salisbury

🐦 MINIATURES DISPLAYS IN THE UNITED STATES 🐦

This state by state listing includes museums and permanent displays of miniatures, dollhouses, dolls and toys nationwide. To assure a pleasant visit, call ahead for specific hours. For information on where to buy miniatures, refer to advertisements in Nutshell News and other miniatures publications, or check your local telephone directory.

ARIZONA
—Carolyn's Dreamland Doll Museum, Box 285, Sedona, AZ 86336.
—Phoenix Art Museum, 1625 N. Central Ave., Phoenix, AZ 85004.

CALIFORNIA
—Angel's Attic, 516 Colorado Ave., Santa Monica, CA 90401.
—Henderson Doll Museum, 40571 Lakeview Dr., Big Bear Lake, CA 92315.
—Hobby City, 1238 S. Beach Blvd., Anaheim, CA 92804.
—Maynard Manor at the Miniature Mart, 1807 Octavia St., San Francisco, CA 94109.
—Mott's Miniatures, Knott's Berry Farm, Buena Park, CA 90620.
—World of Miniature, 1375 South Bascom Ave., San Jose, CA 95128.

COLORADO
—Denver Art Museum, 100 West 14th Ave. Pkwy., Denver, CO 80204.

CONNECTICUT
—Barnham Museum, 820 Main St., Bridgeport, CT 06604.
—Crafty Owl Shop & Doll Museum, 470 Washington Ave., North Haven, CT 06473.
—Historical Museum of the Gunn Memorial Library, Wykeham Rd., Washington, CT 06793.
—Memory Lane Doll & Toy Museum, Olde Mystick Village, Mystic, CT 06355.
—Wilton Heritage Museum, 249 Danbury Rd., Wilton, CT 06897.

DISTRICT OF COLUMBIA
—Smithsonian Institution Museum of History & Technology, 12th & 14th Sts., NW, Washington, DC 20560.
—Washington Dolls' House & Toy Museum, 5236 44th St., NW, Washington, DC 20015.

FLORIDA
—Henry Morrison Flagler Museum, Whitehall Way, PO Box 969, Palm Beach, FL 33480
—Museum of Old Dolls & Toys, 1 mile north of downtown Winter Haven, FL on US Hwy. 17.

GEORGIA
—Enchanted Palace, Hwy. 129, Blairsville, GA 30512.
—Toy Museum of Atlanta, 2800 Peachtree Rd., NE, Atlanta, GA 30305.

ILLINOIS
—Art Institute of Chicago, Michigan Ave. at Adams St., Chicago, IL 60603.
—Klehm's Pink Peony Doll & Mini Museum, 2 East Algonquin Rd., Arlington Heights, IL 60005.
—Museum of Science & Industry, 57th St. & Lake Shore Dr., Chicago, IL 60637.
—Time Was Village Museum, 1325 Burlington Rd., Mendota, IL 61342.

INDIANA
—Children's Museum of Indianapolis, 3000 N. Meridian, Indianapolis, IN 46208.

IOWA
—Museum of Amana History, PO Box 81, Amana, IA 52203.

—Big Doll House Museum, RR 2, State Center, IA 50247.

KENTUCKY
—Gallery of Miniatures, 165 Interchange, Cave City, KY 42127.

MARYLAND
—Potpourri Miniatures, 7811 Montrose Rd., Rockville, MD 20850.

MASSACHUSETTS
—The Children's Museum, 300 Congress St., Boston, MA 02210.
—Children's Museum, 276 Gulf Rd., So. Dartmouth, MA 02748.
—Toy Cupboard Museum, 57 E. George Hill Rd., So. Lancaster, MA 01561.
—Essex Institute, 132 Essex St., Salem, MA 01970.
—Fairbanks Doll Museum, Hall Rd., Sturbridge, MA 01566.
—Plymouth Antiquarian Society, 27 North St., Plymouth, MA 02360.
—Sturbridge Village, Sturbridge, MA 01566
—Wenham Historical Association & Museum, Inc., 132 Main St., Wenham, MA 01984.
—Yesteryear's Museum, Main & River Sts., PO Box 609, Sandwich, MA 02563.

MICHIGAN
—Children's Museum, 67 East Kirby, Detroit, MI 48202.
—Henry Ford Museum, 20900 Oakwood Blvd., Dearborn, MI 48121.

MINNESOTA
—Minnesota Historical Society, 690 Cedar St., St. Paul, MN 55101.

MISSOURI
—Frost Museum of Miniatures, Hwy. 76, 3 miles west of Branson, Star Rt. 1, Box 205, Branson, MO 65616.
—Historic Hermann Museum, Inc., Box 88, Hermann, MO 65041.
—Miniature Museum of Kansas City, 5235 Oak St., Kansas City, MO 64112.
—Missouri Historical Society, Lindell & DeBalivier, St. Louis, MO 63112.

NEW HAMPSHIRE
—The Bunthaus, Main St., Swanzey Center, NH.
—Harrison Gray Otis House, Langdon Mansion, Portsmouth, NH 03801.

NEW JERSEY
—Monmouth County Historical Association, 70 Court St., Freehold, NJ 07728.

NEW MEXICO
—Museum of New Mexico, International Folk Art Museum, 706 Camino Lejo, Santa Fe, NM 87504-2087.
—The Playhouse, Museum of Old Dolls & Toys, 1201 N. Second St., Las Cruces, NM 88005.

NEBRASKA
—Louis B. May Museum, 1643 N. Nye Ave., Fremont, NE 68025.
—Old Brown House Doll Museum, 1421 Ave. F, Gothenburg, NE 69138.

NEW YORK
—Aunt Len's Doll & Toy House, 6 Hamilton Terrace, New York, NY 10031.
—Brooklyn Children's Museum, 145 Brooklyn Ave., Brooklyn, NY 11213.
—Hyde Park Doll Museum, Rt. 9 G, Hyde Park, NY 12538.
—Museum of the City of New York, 5th Ave. & 103rd St., New York, NY 10029.
—The Museum at Stony Brook, 1208 Rt. 25A, Stony Brook, NY 11790.
—New York Historical Society, 170 Central Park W., New York, NY 10024.
—Shaker Museum, Shaker Museum Rd., (1 mile south of Old Chatham), Old Chatham, NY 12136.
—Margaret Woodbury Strong Museum, 700 Allen Creek Rd., Rochester, NY 14618.
—Yorktown Heights Museum, 1974 Commerce, Yorktown Heights, NY 10598.

OHIO
—Allen County Historical Society, 620 W. Market St., Lima, OH 45801.
—Rutherford B. Hayes State Memorial, 1337 Hayes Ave., Fremont, OH 43420.
—Western Reserve Historical Society, 10825 East Blvd., Cleveland, OH 44106.

OKLAHOMA
—Eliza Cruce Doll Museum, Grand St. at East Northwest, Ardmore, OK 63401.

PENNSYLVANIA
—Chester County Historical Society, 225 No. High St., West Chester, PA 19380.
—Dollhouse & Rag Doll Museum, Cresco, PA 18326.
—Happiest Angel Doll Shoppe & Museum, Newfoundland, PA 18445.
—Memory Town, HCR 1, Box 10, Mt. Pocono, PA 18344.
—Mary Merritt Doll Museum, RD 2, Douglasville, PA 19518.
—Perelman Antique Toy Museum, 270 S. Second St., Philadelphia, PA 19106.

RHODE ISLAND
—Newport Historical Society, 82 Touro St., Newport, RI 02840.

SOUTH DAKOTA
—Stuart Castle, Rt. 16, Box 54, Rockerville, SD 57701.

TENNESSEE
—Dulin Gallery of Art, 3100 Kingston Pike, Knoxville, TN 37919.

VERMONT
—Shelbourne Museum, U.S. Rt. 7, Shelbourne, VT 05482.

WASHINGTON
—Museum of History & Industry, 2700 24th Ave., East, Seattle, WA 98112.

WISCONSIN
—Milwaukee County Historical Society, 910 N. Third St., Milwaukee, WI 53203.
—Milwaukee Public Museum, 800 W. Wells St., Milwaukee, WI 53202.
—Mrs. Gray's Doll Museum, Harbor Village, Algoma, WI 54201.

❧ MINIATURES, TOYS AND DOLLS IN EUROPE ❧

Travelers in Europe often serendipitously discover dollhouses and miniatures in the most unusual places. Because these treasures are tucked away off the beaten path, the Publishers acknowledge that some shops, museums or displays may have been overlooked. However, this index should give the touring miniaturist a good departure point in planning his or her travels. To assure a pleasant journey, call or write in advance to verify dates, times, and specific locations. The Publishers thank Sarah Salisbury for her invaluable contributions to this index.

England
Museums and Collections

—The American Museum in Britain. Claverton Manor, near Bath, Avon. Open March-November daily except Monday, 2-5.

—Museum of Costume. Bath, Avon.

—Burrows Toy Museum. York Street, Bath, Avon.

—Luton Museum & Art Gallery. Wardown Park, Luton, Bedfordshire. Open weekdays 10-6, Sunday 2-6, (closed at 5 pm October-March, closed December-January).

—Queen Mary's Dolls' House. Windsor Castle, Eton, Berkshire.

—Cambridge & County Folk Museum. (Two to three dollhouses in poor repair). 2 & 3 Castle Street, Cambridge, Cambridgeshire.

—Preston Hall Museum. Preston Park, Eaglescliffe, Stockton-on-Tees, Cleveland.

—Dolls' House Museum. (Patience Arnold Collection). Prospect House, Kirkstone Road, Ambleside, Cumbria. Open in summer, Wednesday-Friday, 10:30-1, 2-5.

—Alice's Wonderland (Margaret Blackwell Collection). Jennywell, Crosby Ravensworth, Cumbria. (Phone Ravensworth 288 for appointment).

—Hamilton House Toy Museum. 27 Church Street, Ashbourne, Derbyshire. April-October 31; open Saturday 11-5:30, Sunday 2-5:30. Saturday and Sunday all year.

—Museum of Childhood. Sudbury Hall (between Derby and Uttoxeter), Sudbury, Derbyshire.

—Elizabethan House, 70 Fore Street, Totnes, Devon. March-October weekdays 10:30-1, 2-5:30 (reduced hours in winter, phone: 0803 863821).

—Once Upon A Time (Personal collection of Polly Simpson). Ashley Road, Boscombe, Dorset (near Bournemouth). Open daily except Monday and Saturday from 10-5, phone Bournemouth (0202) 33173.

—The Red House Museum. Quay Road, Christchurch, Dorset. Tuesday-Saturday 10-5, Sunday 2-5.

—Sherborne Museum. Abbey Gate House, Sherborne, Dorset. Open April-October weekdays (except Monday) 10:30-12:30, 3-4:30, Sunday 3-5. Winter, Tuesday and Saturday 10:30-12:30, 3-4:30.

—Hove Museum. 19 New Church Road, Hove, East Sussex. Open Monday-Friday 11-1, 2-4:30, Saturday 11-1, 2-5, closed Sunday.

—The Grange Art Gallery & Museum (facing the pond). Rottingdean, East Sussex. Open weekdays 10-5, Sunday 2-5, closed Wednesday.

—Rye Museum. Ypres Tower, Rye, East Sussex. Easter to October 15, weekdays 10:30-1, 2:15-5:30, Sunday 11:30-1, 2:15-5:30.

—Saffron Walden Museum. Museum Street, near Church, Saffron Walden, Essex. Open Summer: weekdays 11-5, Sunday and bank holidays 2:30-5, Winter: weekdays 11-4.

—Stroud & District Museum. Lansdown (Cowle Trust), Stroud, Gloucestershire. Open weekdays 10:30-1, 2-5.

—Toy & Doll Museum (collection of Kay Desmonde) has moved to Studeley Castle (no longer in Syon Park), Winchcombe, Gloucestershire.

—The Curtis Museum. High Street, Alton, Hampshire. Open Monday-Saturday 10-5.

—Uppark. Near Petersfield, Hampshire.

—Playthings Past Museum (Collection of Betty Cadbury). "Beaconwood," Bromsgrove, Rednal (near Birmingham), Hereford & Worcester. Open by written application for appointment; no children under 12.

—Mrs. Gondolphin's Toy Collection. Canterbury, Kent.

—Penshurst Toy Museum, Penshurst Place, Tonbridge, Kent.

—The Precinct Toy Collection. 38 Harnet Street, Sandwich, Kent. Open Easter to end of September, weekdays 10-5, Sunday 2-5, October: Saturday and Sunday only, 2-5.

—Tunbridge Wells Museum. Civic Center, Mount Pleasant, Tunbridge Wells, Kent. Monday-Friday 10-5:30 (except bank holidays), and Saturday 9:30-5.

—The Judges' Lodgings Museum of Childhood (Barry Elder doll collection). Church Street, Lancaster, Lancashire. Open Easter-October daily 2-5.

—London Museum. London Wall, London EC2Y 5HN. Open Tuesday-Saturday 10-6, Sunday 2-6.

—Victoria & Albert Museum. Cromwell Road, South Kensington, London SW7 2RI. Open Monday-Saturday 10-6, Sunday 2:30-6.

—Bethnal Green Museum (branch of Victoria & Albert Museum). Cambridge Heath Road, London E2 9PA. Open Monday-Saturday (except Friday) 10-6, Sunday 2:30-6.

—Pollock's Toy Museum. 1 Scala Street (at Goodge Street), London. Open Monday-Saturday 10-5.

—Monks Hall Museum. 42 Wellington Road, Eccles, Salford, Greater Manchester. Open Monday-Friday 10-6, Saturday 10-5.

—Queen's Park Art Gallery. Queen's Park, Harpurhey, Manchester 9. Open March-October weekdays 10-6, Sunday 2-6 (open 12-6 from May to August).

—Botanic Gardens Museum. Churchtown, Southport, Merseyside. Open weekdays 10-6 (winter 10-5), Sunday 2-5 (dusk in winter), closed Monday.

—Museum of Social History. 27 King Street (next to St. George's Guildhall), King's Lynn, Norfolk. Open Tuesday-Saturday 10-5.

—Wallington Hall (National Trust). Cambo, Morpeth, Northumberland, (near Hexham).

—Museum of Costume & Textiles. Castlegate, Nottingham, Nottinghamshire.

—The Rotunda (collection of Vivien Greene). Grove House, 44 Iffley Turn (across from the school), Oxford, Oxfordshire. Open May-September, Sunday 2:15-5:15, at other times by written arrangements for 12 or more people, no children under 16.

—Somerset County Museum. Taunton Castle, Taunton, Somerset. Open Monday-Friday 10-5.

—Museum of Mr. and Mrs. Harrison Burgess (Dollhouse nine feet long, 14 rooms and stables). 2 High Street, Axbridge, Somerset. Open Easter-October Saturday, Sunday, bank holidays, some weekdays.

—Warwick Doll Museum. Oken's House on Castle Street, Warwick, Warwickshire. Open weekdays 10-6, Sunday 2:30-5.

—Bantock House. Bantock Park, Wolverhampton, West Midlands. Open Monday-Friday 10-7, Saturday 10-6, Sunday 2-5.

—Dolls House Museum. 23 High Street, Arundel, West Sussex.

—Worthing Museum. Chapel Road, Worthing, West Sussex. Open weekdays 10-6 (October-March 10-5).

—Pembroke Palace (formerly known as Wilton Dolls' House). Wilton (near Salisbury), Wiltshire.

—Longleat House. Warminster, Wiltshire.

—Nunnington Hall (Carlisle collection). Twenty miles north of York, Yorkshire (on banks of River Rye).

—Castle Museum. Tower Street, York, North Yorkshire. Open weekdays 10-5, Sunday 2-5.

England
Shops

—Pollock's. Covent Garden, London.

—The Dolls' House Toys Ltd. (Michal Morse). 29 The Market, Covent Garden, London.

—The Singing Tree (Thalia Sanders & Anne Griffith). 69 New Kings Road, London. Open Monday-Saturday 10-5:30 (except Thursday 10-1).

—Kay Desmonde's Shop. 17 Kensington Church Walk (off Kensington High Street), London.

—Bumble (Mary Isaacs). 2 Strelley Way, London.

—Constance Eileen King's Shop. Camden Passage, Islington, London. Open Wednesday and Saturday.

—Fiddly Bits (Hillary Swallow). 24 King Street, Knutsford, Cheshire.

—Dolls House Corner. Colliton Craft Market, Dorchester, Dorset.

—Miniature Interiors (Miren Tong). 62 Kiln Ride, Wokingham, Berkshire.

—Polly Flinders (Wendy Hunter-Smith). 46 London Road, Reigate, Surrey.

—Sussex Crafts (Peter Warwick). 26 Brighton Road, Crawley, Sussex.

—The Mulberry Bush (Lionel and Ann Barnard). 25 Trafalgar Square, Brighton, Sussex.

—Miniature World. 37 Princess Victoria Street, Clifton, Bristol, Avon.

—Chalfont Fine Arts. Chalfont St. Giles, Buckinghamshire.

—Minimus. 72 Beche Road, Cambridge, Cambridgeshire.

—Halfpenny Workshops. Torrington Street, Bideford, Devon.

❧ MINIATURES, TOYS AND DOLLS IN EUROPE ❧

England
Miniature Villages

—Bourton-on-the-Water. (behind New Old Inn), Cottswold.

—Beconscot. Beaconsfields.

—Babbacombe Village. Torquay, Devon.

—Merrivale Model Village. Great Yarmouth, Norfolk.

—Tucktonia. Tuckton Park (1 mile from Christchurch Station), nr. Bournemouth, Dorset.

Ireland, Scotland & Wales
Museums

—Museum of Childhood. 38 High Street, Edinburgh, Scotland.

—The Dolls House (Mrs. Gwen Price's private collection). Wrexham, Clwyd, Wales.

—The Polly Edge Collection. Laugharne, Dyfed, Wales.

—Llandudno Doll Museum & Model Railway. Masonic Street, Llandudno, Gwynedd, North Wales. Open daily 10-1, 2-:530, Sunday 2-5:30 from Easter through the end of September.

—Penrhyn Castle. Between Conway Castle and Caernarfon Castle, near Bangor, Gwynedd, North Wales.

—Museum of Childhood. Water Street, Menai Bridge, Gwynedd, North Wales. Open Easter-October, Monday-Saturday 10-5:30, Sunday 1-5.

—Museum of Childhood. National Museum, Kildare Street, Dublin, Ireland.

—Arreton Manor. Arreton, Isle of Wight.

France
Museums

—Musee des Arts Decoratifs (in The Louvre). 107-109 Rue de Rivoli, Paris, closed Mondays.

—Jardin d'Acclimation. Bois de Boulogne, 75116 Paris, (showing La Grande Maison des Poupees, 25' by 15').

—Musee de Jouet. Poissy (in an old abbey outside Paris). Take train from Gare St. Lazare. Closed Monday and Tuesday.

—Versailles. Showing a miniature Louis XIV bed chamber and the Stairway of the Ambassadors.

—Musee d'Unterlinden (in a Dominican convent).

—Musee Alsacien. Strasbourg.

—Musee de l'Oeuvre de Notre Dame. Strasbourg.

France
Shops

—Au Nain Bleu (Mr. and Mrs. Labbey). 408 Fauborg St. Honore, Paris 75008.

—Polichinelle/Scaramouche (Francois Theimer). 14 Rue Andre del Sarte (near Sacre Coeur), Paris 75018.

—Napthaline. 9 Allee Riesener, Le Louvre des Antiquairies, Place du Palais Royal, Paris.

—Christian Bailly. 19 Allee Riesener, Le Louvre des Antiquaires, 2 Rue de Palais Royal, Paris 75001.

—Le Petit Chateau. 126 Rue de Chateau, Paris 14.

—Jacqueline Capdeville. Dale Photographic, 17 Rue Andre del Sarte, Paris.

—Maison de Cochon-du-Lait (M. and Mme. Neppel Roland). Place de Marche aux Cochons de Lait, Strasbourg 67000.

—Aux Merveilles de la Cathedrale. 9, Place de la Cathedrale, Strasbourg 67000.

Germany
Museums

—Speilzeugmuseum der Stadt Nurnberg (City of Nuremberg Toy Museum). Karlstrasse 13, Nuremberg, (Lydia Bayer collection). Closed Monday.

—Germanisches National Museum. Corner of Kartausergasse & Kornmarkt 1, Nuremberg.

—Historisches Museum. Frankfurt-on-Main.

—Heimatmuseum, Uberlingon.

—Stadtische Kunstsmmlungen. Augsburg.

—Maxmiliams Museum. Augsburg.

—Altonaer Museum. Hamburg.

—Landesgewerbe Museum. Stuttgart.

—Triberg Local Museum. Outside Baden Baden.

—Munchner Stadt Museum. Munich. Closed Mondays.

—Museum der Stadt Ulm. Ulm.

—Schlossmuseum. Arnstadt, East Germany.

—Schloss Museum. Berlin.

The Netherlands
Museums

—Rijksmuseum. Stadhouderskade 42, Amsterdam.

—The Frans Hals Museum, Groot Heiligland 62, Haarlem.

—Stedelike Museum. Haarlem.

—Central Museum. Agnietinstraat 1, Utrecht.

—Gemeente Museum. Arnhem.

—Gemeente Museum. Stadhouderslaan 41, The Hague.

—Costume Museum. Lange Vijverberg 14 & 15, The Hague.

—Speelgoed en Blikmuseum (formerly De Drie Haringen Museum).

—Rotterdam Historisch Museum. Rotterdam.

—Museum Mr. Simon Van Gijn. Dordrecht.

—Cosmorama Miniatura. Valkenburg.

—Westfries Museum. Hoorn.

—Stedelijk Museum. Alkmar.

—Stedelijk Museum. Gouda.

The Netherlands
Miniature Villages

—Madurodam. Haringade 175, The Hague ('s Gravenhage).

The Netherlands
Shops

—Grote Market antique section. Rotterdam.

—Rachel Roet. Spekstraat 2 (off the Denneweg), Den Haag.

—De Bijenkorf (a department store), Merkelbach (a toy store), or Waterlooplein (a flea market). Amsterdam.

Switzerland
Museums

—Toy Museum of Zurich (Franz Carl Weber collection). Fortunagasse 15, Zurich.

—Schweizerischen Landesmuseum. (Behind the station), Zurich.

—Schweizerischen Museum fur Volkskunde. Basel.

—Kirschgarten Museum. Elisabethenstrasse 27, Basel.

—Wettsteinhaus. Baselstrasse 34, Riehen (near Basel).

—Spielzug and Dorfmuseum. Riehen (near Basel).

INDEX TO PHOTOGRAPHS

INDEX TO ARTISANS

INDEX TO ARTISANS

❧ INDEX TO ARTISANS ❧

THE END